TROUBLE WITH
THE LAW

TROUBLE WITH THE LAW

THE LAW

A WESTERN DOUBLE

UZZIAH MOUNTAIN MAN
BOOK THREE

J.J. BONHAM

WOLFPACK
PUBLISHING
— EST 2013 —

Trouble with the Law: A Western Double
Paperback Edition
Copyright © 2025 (As Revised) by J.J. Bonham

Wolfpack Publishing
1707 E. Diana Street
Tampa, FL 33610

www.wolfpackpublishing.com

Paperback ISBN 979-8-89567-779-7
Ebook ISBN 979-8-89567-778-0

TROUBLE WITH
THE LAW

TROUBLE WITH
THE LAW

1

They had ridden down to the trading post called Fort Saint Vrain. Immanuel was certain they could still get good prices for their pelts there, even though the fashion for gentlemen had turned to silk. While he was haggling with the master of the post, Jean Baptiste, Uzziah went to the counter where mail was sent from and mail received. They fully expected to run into Jean Baptiste, but Uzziah's memory of how he'd treated Leah was still fresh in his mind. Not that Uzziah didn't want to talk with him, it was just weird in some way.

"How can I help ya?" the man behind the counter asked Uzziah.

"Ya got any mail fer me?"

"I ain't a fortune teller, who are you?"

"Oh, sorry, Uzziah Ferguson O'Bannon."

The man went back and started rifling through the stacks of mail.

"This might take a while," he said over his shoulder.

"I'll be over there, just shout out," Uzziah said, walking back over to where Immanuel was haggling.

"I hear that the young, and vibrant Miss Leah has found a match in the mountains," Baptiste said to Uzziah.

O'Bannon looked at his partner, not sure how he felt about that news getting out.

"*Excusez-moi*," Baptists said and left the counter, going back into the store.

"Did ya tell him where he could find her, too?" O'Bannon asked, sounding piqued.

"Don't get yer old lady panties in a wad," Immanuel said, smiling at Uzziah.

"Ya think it's funny, don't ya, well, it ain't funny when a man thrashes a woman, I don't care how far in the past it was."

"Ya never hit a woman?"

Uzziah stood straighter and simply looked at Immanuel. "I will ferget ya asked me that."

"Ya forgettin' 'cause ya have, or because ya haven't?"

Uzziah was about to answer with some volume, but Jean Baptiste came back. He rubbed his hands together. "I love it when we bargain," he said.

"Well, I'll love it if the price is right," Immanuel offered.

"Here's what my partner in the back and myself think all yer pelts are worth," he said, sliding a piece of paper across the counter. Uzziah picked it up fast.

"That was meant fer me," Immanuel said.

"We's partners," Uzziah said as he looked at the paper and smiled. "Seems about right," he said, then slid the paper across the counter to his partner.

Immanuel put on his readers he'd gotten the last year, and squinted at it.

"O'Bannon!" the man at the mail counter called his name.

As Uzziah sauntered over to the mail counter, he could hear many curses coming from his partner, Immanuel. Well, he kind of thought the price was all right, but obviously Immanuel didn't agree. What was new?

The man at the mail counter handed him an envelope.

Uzziah unfolded the envelope, which was actually the letter, and read:

Dear Son,

I am not glad to include you intwo the news of yer mother's illness. She took sic a few weeks ago, and has been rendered feeble by whatever had struck her down. She asked me too ask ya to come home. I am afraid she isn't long fer this age ore world. She says she luvs ya more than life itself, and would wish too sea you a time once more befour she passes thru the vail.

Affectionately, Yer Pa,
Sean Wilson O'Bannon

Uzziah read the letter through again, and once more for good measure. He could hear Baptiste and Immanuel James Jones arguing in the background.

Right now, it didn't seem important to him what they got for the pelts. He just needed to get home. He wandered over to the counter where Baptiste was swearing in French, the only word he could make out was *merde*, which he thought was the French word for *shite*.

Immanuel stood there listening to the man swearing in a foreign tongue and was smiling. Finally, the tirade ceased and Jean Baptiste threw the piece of paper back into Immanuel's face.

The crumpled-up piece of paper bounced off his nose, and Immanuel laughed. Uzziah knew the difference between a real Jones's laugh and a faked one—this was real. Baptiste turned and stomped back into the backroom.

"He's tryin' to rob us, it's as simple as that," Immanuel said. "I say we take the furs to St. Louis, and sell them, there."

"I agree," Uzziah said, and his partner of the past five years turned to him as if he'd said, *Let's shoot Baptiste.*

"What'd ya say!?!?

"Let's go."

"You mean it?"

"We're partners, ain't we, if ya say go to St. Louis, we go to St. Louis."

"But the law?"

"What about the law?" Uzziah asked, smiling.

Immanuel hugged his rather robust partner and lifted him off the floor. "God, sometimes, I really luv ya, ya know, really, really love ya!?"

"I do, now if I could become earthbound, once again?"

Immanuel put Uzziah down. "Really, y'all go, regardless of the danger?"

"We'll figure somethin' out by the time we gits there."

"Yer right, yer always bloody well right, well, I won't go that fer, but this time, ya are!"

———

They traveled north to where the Missouri River, the Mighty Mo, ran through the Dakota territories. Immanuel had told him they were going to a large village where at least a thousand natives of the Mandan Nation lived. It was there, Immanuel had taken his only wife, a Mandan squaw named Chinoa, which meant White Dove. Of course, since she had died, Immanuel had never spoken her name, which was the custom of all natives. As Uzziah was being told this, he had a nagging memory of Immanuel saying he'd taken another squaw from another tribe, but who was keeping records and who accusing whom of what?

Uzziah had never been to this village, and as they traveled there, he could only imagine what it would be like. They camped for two weeks out from Vrain Outpost, and Uzziah had biscuits in his Dutch oven and bacon frying in the pan. Immanuel was out hunting, and as the wind blew from the east, it brought the smell of the prairie grasses with it. Uzziah thought about Flying Feathers, whom they had left with the cabins before starting out for the post where they had hoped to sell their pelts.

He knew she was self-sufficient, that their being there at the cabins made little to no difference to her at all. With the bow and arrows she had made, she was, in fact, a better hunter than either of them. But still, he had spent many a winter night with her warming his bed, and even though she had the habit of closing her eyes when he entered her, and not opening them again, until he was through, he knew she loved him in her own way. Well, maybe she did, then again, maybe it was her way of pretending he was somebody else. Who knew?

There was the sound of someone behind him, and he whirled around, thinking he was about to be set on by an enemy.

"Yer gonna get yerself kilt, day-dreamin' thataway," Immanuel said. He had a young antelope over his shoulder, and its blood had drained down on his deer-skin shirt. He dropped the antelope and a puff of dust rose up and was taken away by the east wind.

"Where'd ya find that one?" Uzziah asked.

"He was grazing peacefully with his brothers and sisters."

"This is almost ready."

"I'll skin it quick like, then cut off some steaks." Immanuel had learned long ago that the best antelope meat was spoiled if it wasn't skinned quickly after the kill and the meat cooked immediately. Before the Dutch oven was opened and the biscuits ready, there were two antelope steaks skewered on willow sticks and dripping their tasty juices onto the fire.

They sat quietly after one of the best meals they had had in a long time.

"Maybe we could take the rest of the meat to the Mandans?" Uzziah asked.

"Nah, it'll spoil in another hour, unless we got ice, and I don't see any of that around. I'll drag it out a ways from camp and we'll let the cayotes take it fer their meal."

"How much further to their camp?"

"Well, I'd say another two or three days of hard ridin' and we'll be there," Immanuel said.

"I remember yer squaw wife was from this village, right?"

"That's so, wonder if her old man is still chief?"

"Hope so," Uzziah said, wondering if Immanuel had ever been married to anyone—white or red?

"Me, too, brother. We'll get the real welcome of the Mandans ifn he is."

They sat after they'd eaten and Uzziah had cleaned as best he could without water, the utensils. He used the sand in the dry creek bed, and it did just fine.

After that, the sun was down and the deep indigo of the east was spreading westward as they lit their pipes.

"Ya lookin' forward to seeing them again?" Uzziah asked.

"Brother, how many times I gots to tell ya, Injuns are notional."

"Yeah, but you said these Mandans were peaceful farmers," Uzziah objected.

"Yeah, but it's been a while since I seen 'em, they might have taken a different notion about the white man since then."

———

It took four more days, but on the fourth and final day of their journey, they made a rise in the plains, and down below them was the Mandan village. The mud huts had holes in the tops where smoke curled skyward.

Children were managing the herd of horses by the river. The huts were fairly close together, and some children had already climbed up on the edge of the roofs and were playing. Tall poles were stuck in the ground throughout the village. Some had white banners hanging down from them, some black, and some had the images of a man hanging from the top, not really hanging, more topping off the poles.

"Well, there's only one way to see if they're peaceful, come on," Immanuel said as he put his heels into the side of his horse and pulled the rope that was attached to a mule. The other beast of burden was their donkey, which had the strips of the cross on her back. Her name didn't matter anymore. Uzziah thought they'd called her Jenny, but whatever her name was, she went where she wanted to go, smelled what she wanted to smell, and if they got too far off, she'd run to catch up.

She'd gotten the habit by following Samson, the draft horse mare that Immanuel and Uzziah tried to set free, but followed them everywhere. She had wowed an Apache village and been given to the young Geronimo, but somehow, she had ended up back with them in the mountains. The Jesus donkey loved that old mare, and she followed it until one trip, neither showed up at their camp, and when they went looking, the donkey was curled up beside the dead mare, who, they guessed, had simply run out of time.

They didn't bury the mare, but cut hairs from its mane and tail and read the Bible over the dead body. They had to tie a rope to the Jesus donkey to get her to leave, she was such a faithful friend. She brayed throughout that night and would have returned to the body the next morning if they hadn't dragged her home.

"Is she comin'?" Immanuel asked Uzziah who was looking back at her.

"Maybe?"

"Fair enough," Immanuel said.

The mule was held by Immanuel, he couldn't be let off for a bit before he'd take off and they'd have to catch him. He brayed loudly as they came down off the rise, and that was like an alarm. All the children on the roofs came down and ran into their mud huts, and the boys by the river, the Mighty Mo, gathered the horses in case they were needed, and about twenty-some men, Mandan warriors, came out away from the village and walked toward the horses. They mounted up their ponies, and turning them from the river, they rode out toward the two men and the mule.

They rode hard and fast, and yet they did not make threatening noises, or yell, or anything. Uzziah was so used to that that this silent rendezvousing disturbed him more than the other. Finally, about twenty yards from them, the Mandans came to a halt, all in a line.

"We'll stop, too," Immanuel said in a whisper. The mule brayed again, maybe he was glad to be stopping, who knew with mules.

The Mandans all grinned, and some actually smiled openly at this.

"Good thing you no sneak up on us," a warrior said who was tall in the saddle. He had two braids down the front of his shirt, and two feathers topping off his head. His braids were tight, but the front of his hair was shorter and pulled to the right side so that it blew in the slight breeze that was traveling among them. He had the typical Injun nose bent from the eyes down to the mouth. Full lips and a strong chin, and he was sort of smiling.

"Mule give battle cry," Immanuel said, and Uzziah wished he hadn't used the word *battle*.

The one who had spoken repeated what Immanuel had said, and all the others grunted in reply.

"What...need here?"

Immanuel went into his sign language, which was fast and evidently fairly good. He went on for a long while, and the reactions of the Mandans on the horses were varied. At one point, they all smiled, and then it seemed they would almost cry, then they grunted and Immanuel had stopped.

Uzziah then noticed that one of the men was, or at least seemed to be, listening closer than the rest. He thought it original for them to come out to greet strangers with so many. Finally, he spoke in Mandan to the others. They listened as he gave an oration of sorts. When he was finished, Uzziah guessed that Immanuel had heard enough to remember what he'd learned from his squaw wife, if he actually had one?

He spoke to them haltingly at first, then got more proficient as he went on. The man rode ahead of the others and up to Immanuel's horse so he could hear better, Uzziah guessed.

"Your Mandan is terrible, but still, I understand you. You had taken a Mandan wife, Chinoa, White Dove, in your language, where is she?"

Uzziah thanked the stars above, he would never have said the wife's name if the Mandan had not thought that she was still alive.

"She whose name I cannot speak is no longer with us," Immanuel said, bowing his head in reverence.

The man looked at him and studied his posture of grief, which must have impressed him somewhat.

"I am Sheheke," he said. "My father chief of the Mandans many, many, many moons before the Lewis and the Clarke."

"Your father went to Washington to see Thomas Jefferson, didn't he?"

"Many moons before he back. He with spirits now, I chief. What you want?"

"We smoke first, Sheheke," Immanuel said, and then the other men started laughing and pointing.

Immanuel turned, and it was the little donkey with the cross on his back, running fast to catch up. He came up beside Uzziah and stopped.

"Good girl," Uzziah said and she brayed.

"Much fun, come and smoke."

Immanuel rode back and whispered to Uzziah, "He said, 'You have much fun with you.' I hope that fun don't include torture." He pulled the mule's rope and, braying, he walked behind Immanuel with the Mandans laughing a lot more now.

2

They rode to the middle of the camp, there were a lot of mud huts. Children ran beside them, and both the mountain men thought that was good. When they stopped at the largest of the huts, Sheheke got off his horse, and it was taken away for him. He opened the flap to the hut and waited for the two mountain men.

Uzziah looked at the pelts and sure hoped that they would be okay. Immanuel shrugged as if to say, who knows, and they both went inside.

Darkness caused them to be momentarily blind, except for the small fire in the middle, whose smoke escaped through the top hole. Finally, they saw that Sheheke was seated and he gestured to the floor opposite him. They sat there on the other side of the fire as a woman was preparing a meal of some sort. The light from the hole in the top struck her on the face as she turned and smiled at Uzziah and he did a double-take. Her eyes were the color of the Missouri, blue, so blue. He would have to ask Immanuel about that later. She stirred the concoction in the pot and left the fire.

By this time, Sheheke had brought out a red stone pipe with a long wooden stem to draw on. He lit the pipe, held it up to the four directions, and, taking a puff, he passed it to Immanuel. He smoked it without the ceremony of the four directions, and Uzziah imagined that particular motion was for the chief alone.

After they had smoked, whatever was in the pot on the fire was served to the three men. It was a stew of deer meat, probably. Whatever it was, it was delicious, and Uzziah felt like asking for seconds, but held himself back. He knew that traditionally, the women ate after the men, and if the stew was gone, they would be out of luck.

After they ate, Sheheke sat back and lit the pipe again. This time, the pipe was different, so Uzziah pulled his own pipe out and lit it. Immanuel looked at Uzziah as if he'd committed a faux pas, but Sheheke spoke up.

"May I try your tobacco?"

"Certainly," Uzziah said as he handed his pouch around and Sheheke smelled it first.

"Mum," he said in appreciation of its aroma.

"Please," Uzziah said, making the motion for taking some, and Sheheke did just that. Then he tapped out the burning tobacco in his pipe into the fire, and stuffed it with Uzziah's tobacco and lit it.

He blew the smoke with a smile on his face over the fire, and the smoke traveled up with the smoke from the fire.

"I like this," he said, smiling, then added, "You want to sell pelts?"

"No," Uzziah said, and the smile on Sheheke's face disappeared.

"Well, maybe not," Immanuel said, and the chief smiled again.

"We will talk price later," Sheheke said, and that was that.

———————

There was a celebration in the Mandan village that night. They left the teepee and sat around the big fire. Corn and squash, which they had grown in their immense fields, were roasted over the fire, and the squashes were opened up, the seeds taken out, and honey poured into them. They were butternut squash, and Uzziah watched as the men put their hands wrapped in leather around the handles of the squash and ate them with the honey running down their chins. He had never enjoyed squash much before and found that this way, it tasted like nothing he'd ever had before. They were served a coolish drink, which was opaque and yellow.

"It's corn beer, be careful, my friend," Immanuel had said to Uzziah. "This was the beer that got me married to the woman whose name I cannot speak."

Uzziah watched as Immanuel then began to sip the beer. His expression changed into a face that Uzziah was sure he'd never seen before. The past must have come rushing back upon him as he remembered a similar celebration and the wonderfully beautiful Chinoa serving him the beverage which would lead him into her teepee.

A half hour later, Uzziah looked up and was aghast

that Immanuel was singing a Mandan song with the other braves, and dancing with abandon around the fire. His face was lit from within, and he realized that the warning that Immanuel had given him had not been heeded by the warning giver.

The rest of the night was a blur to Immanuel as he threw tomahawks, ran races, and rode barback along the river's edge. Once the horse and he fell into the river and only the horse came up.

Mandan braves ran up and down the riverbank as they yelled in Mandan. Uzziah was concerned, then he saw the tiny figure of Immanuel on the other shore screaming something in Mandan and the braves all laughed until they couldn't stand.

Immanuel then jumped into the Mighty Mo way upstream and let the river take him back to the camp of Sheheke. He was greeted as a returning warrior, and then Uzziah lost track of him and the time.

When the false dawn was just etching its way into the east, Uzziah awakened. He was sitting by the fire, but had lain back and, curling up, he'd gone to sleep. Someone had placed a Mandan blanket on him. He looked around and many of the celebrating warriors were laid out, all sleeping in various positions of them having passed out. He laughed to himself until he looked and noticed the pelts, which had been unloaded from the mule and the donkey, were gone.

Finally, Immanuel came from one of the huts, Uzziah did not want to know whom he'd been with, he just hoped he wasn't married this time. He tumbled to the water's edge and, lying prone, stuck his head into the cold water. Bringing it back out, he shook his head like a dog would, and sat by the river, taking handfuls of water and drinking them.

"Our pelts are gone," Uzziah said, standing beside Immanuel.

"Yeah, I seem to remember something about a trade," he said and looked about. There was an enormous raft that had been pulled up on shore. It had a tent-like structure on it, and poles to navigate the downward movement of the Mighty Mo, to keep the raft in the middle of the current. There was enough room on it for the two of them, all their things, and the stock.

"I'm not sure, but I may have traded all the pets for that raft," Immanuel said as he turned and regurgitated into the river.

"You what?"

"I only think that's what I've done," he said, wiping his beard and mouth off and washing the detritus off in the water.

"Where are the pelts?" Uzziah asked.

"Who knows?"

"You'd better know, and you'd better know now!" Uzziah was mad as a hatter. He'd seen Immanuel like this before, and each time, it had brought them grief.

"It's an ill wind that blows no good," Immanuel said.

"Yeah, well, we do have a way to get to St. Louis. But, oh wait, nothing to sell once we get there," Uzziah crooned.

"Yeah, well, there you go," Immanuel said, lying down by the river.

"Did you marry anyone?" Uzziah asked.

"As a matter of fact..."

"No! Not really?"

"No, I thought about it, but she was so ugly compared to she whose name I cannot speak."

A Mandan boy had come up and sat beside Immanuel.

"Hello there," Immanuel said, and to his surprise, the boy spoke almost perfect English.

"You take me, St. Louis," he said and smiled.

"What?" Immanuel asked him, then recognizing him, he said, "I promised you that last night, didn't I?"

Uzziah slapped his forehead with the flat of his hand and regretted it immediately. Wow, did that hurt!

"You, me, St. Louis," the boy said, "I am Sahale, it mean above in a high place."

"What about yer parents?" Uzziah asked him.

"They dead. I am...how say, orphan."

"Do you know what I did with the beaver pelts, Sahale?" Immanuel asked.

"Yes."

"Well, where are they?"

"You, me, St. Louis," Sahale said.

"He's got a one-track mind," Uzziah said.

"You tell ole Immanuel where the pelts are and we'll take you St. Louis," Immanuel announced.

"Immanuel, no!" Uzziah stepped in front of Immanuel to make his point clear.

Immanuel winked and looked back at the boy, "So, do you know where they're at?"

"I show," he said, and Immanuel stood up with Uzziah right behind him.

"Down river at big bend."

"How do you know this?" Uzziah asked, curious as to the boy's truthfulness.

"You, me, St. Louis," Sahale said, "I show."

"Oh hell," Uzziah said, "what do we have to lose? I'll go get the horses."

"Just the horses, I'm pretty sure that was the mule we ate last night," Immanuel said.

Uzziah looked at Immanuel with disgust, then, turning, emptied the contents of his stomach.

Immanuel looked hard at Sahale. "If you lie," he said, and he drew his thumb across his throat.

"No lie. You, me, St. Louis."

Uzziah left and returned with the horses. Shadow was quite glad to see Uzziah.

"Well, come on," Immanuel said as they walked down to the large raft.

They pushed the raft onto the river, and only had it stay there by a rope which was tied to a stout tree. Uzziah rode Shadow out to the raft, and he was tied to a post in the middle of the raft. They had a bit more trouble with Immanuel's horse, who wanted to, but did not trust the footing on the raft. Uzziah untied Shadow and rode him into the river, while Immanuel rode his horse up beside him.

"Now, we get 'um both up at the same time, then Sahale cuts the rope," Uzziah said.

"You got that, boy?" Immanuel asked the boy who was standing in the river with a satchel on his back and a large knife in his hand, it was probably the only things he owned.

"Horses up, cut rope," he said and smiled.

They kicked their horses up, and Immanuel's horse lagged just a bit, but got up just as Sahale jumped up on the raft, then cut the rope. The raft spun out into deeper waters and both men had to dismount and hold the reins firmly. The horses whinnied a bit, then settled down.

Off on the shore, their donkey, the Jesus donkey with the two black stripes on his back making a cross at the shoulders, thought nothing of what was going on. He ran up, the sawbuck still on his back, and seeing them on the raft, jumped in and swam behind the enormous raft.

The entire village hadn't noticed what was going on down by the shore. It was early in the morning. The boys who kept the horses for the tribe ran back to tell what they had seen.

The raft was picking up speed and Uzziah and Immanuel had to maneuver the poles to keep them more or less in the middle of the river. Shadow felt so comfortable, he lay down on the grass which Sahale had brought up from the fields, and fairly soon, Immanuel's horse did the same.

"Who knew?" Immanuel yelled at Uzziah, who simply smiled big and kept poling the boat into the middle.

"There," yelled Sahale as he pointed down the river.

Up ahead, about three hundred yards, the river did a left turn on itself. It was what cowboys called an oxbow. They poled their way to the right, and when the river bent, they ran the large raft up on the beach.

"Come, I show!" Sahale yelled as he jumped from the raft and ran through the water to the shore. The two men secured the raft as best they could and ran after the boy. They had placed the pelts in a cave, made from when the water ran higher, and had cut out the cave.

"How do we get 'em to the raft?" Immanuel asked.

"Look!" Uzziah said, and there was Jenny, coming with quick steps up toward where they were. The sawbuck saddle on her back was dripping wet.

"I'm guessing we didn't eat Jenny," Uzziah said.

"Good thing, huh," Immanuel said as he started loading her up, and then they went back to the beach. The raft had been pulled out a bit from the mooring they had set it in, and Sahale had to jump into the water and bring the rope back to the men, who, with the help of Jenny, pulled it back on the beach.

They loaded the pelts into the tent erected close to the middle of the raft, and Jenny started braying.

"We're gonna take ya, girl, we will!" Immanuel said, reassuring her as he coaxed her onto the raft.

"Look!" Uzziah said as he pointed downriver, and there in the middle of the stream, there were half a dozen canoes coming their way, and they each had three Mandans in them. They pushed the raft back out, and it made the curves of the ox bow, but slowly. As they looked back, they realized they were going to be caught by the warriors.

Uzziah laid on the raft and loaded his Hawken.

"We gonna kill 'em?" Immanuel asked as he lay down beside his partner.

"Sorta," Uzziah said, and the Hawken exploded. Immanuel looked, and the front canoe was hit just at the waterline and began to sink.

"You, cheesy bastard," Immanuel said as he laid down and shot a hole in the next closest canoe. Mandans were abandoning canoes left and right and swimming ashore. They had not bothered to bring anything but bows and arrows, and the other canoes let fly with high arrows which careened down upon them.

Uzziah ran over and laid on top of Shadow, and Immanuel just kept loading and shooting. Fairly soon, the arrows fell short and they were safe.

Sahale was laughing so hard, he fell over.

"You think that's funny, don't ya?" Uzziah asked him.

"Father swim like bear," Sahale said, and continued to laugh, pointing at one of the last of the Mandans as he made his way to shore.

"Orphan, my arse," Immanuel said picking the boy up over his head. "I hope ya can swim like a cub," and he threw the boy overboard.

He splashed and disappeared below the surface.

"What ifn he can't swim?" Uzziah asked.

Sahale surfaced with a sputter and yelled back at them, "You, me, St. Louis!" Then, getting his bearings, he swam toward the shore. As he made the shore, he shot them the finger.

"Hey, I didn't know they did that like us!?" Uzziah said.

"Young son, they been doing that since Diogenes flipped Demosthenes off back in Athens four hundred years before Christ."

"How do you know somethin' like that?"

"Books, they're amazin', if and only if, ya read 'em."

———

They drifted sometimes slowly, then more rapidly, the rest of the day. The occasional pole was needed to keep them in the middle of the downward-flowing stream. Jenny had her sawbuck saddle taken off and settled down lying flat between the two horses. From time to time, the horses would get up and blow, and by sunset, they were anxious to get ashore. They pulled onto a beach on an island quite away from either shore, and they let the horses and Jenny off. They ran all over the island, and at one time, Uzziah was scared they'd swim to the shore, but Immanuel reminded him they had the hay. And yet, Uzziah could see the full and luscious prairie grasses along the shore. They harvested plenty of it off the island before supper, and the horses and Jenny came back, were hobbled, then enjoyed their evening meal of island grasses, as Uzziah fixed supper for Immanuel and himself.

3

They got up early the next morning and let the horse and Jenny run around. Uzziah figured if they could get the horses and the donkey worn out, then they might fare better on the raft during the day. By the time the sun was coming up, they were well underway. Both the mountain men were amazed at how the horses had adapted to being on the large raft. Fairly soon, after launching, they all settled down to the tall grass which Uzziah had harvested for them.

"Do ya feel bad about throwing the boy overboard?" Uzziah asked his partner.

"'Bout as bad as I feel when I pull a splinter out of my hand. He didn't belong with us, and if he hadn't said something about the way his pa swam, we might forever be considered outlaws in the Mandan nation."

"Well, since we didn't pay for the raft, and evidently you promised the pelts as payment for this rather large raft, we still might be considered so," Uzziah said.

"Well, I've thought of a way around that very problem," Immanuel said.

"Oh?"

"We'll get down as far as the paddle steamers come up, around Fort Benton, then leave the raft there, and take the paddle boat to St. Louis."

"Well, how will the Mandans get it back?" Uzziah asked.

"I'll pay for the next boat goin' up the river to drag it along, shouldn't cost much," Immanuel said.

"Do ya think that'll work?"

"Who knows, we stole the damn thing and ought to try, don't ya think?"

Uzziah didn't answer, he thought the whole thing disgusting. Whenever Immanuel had too much to drink, he was always getting himself—and since Uzziah was his partner, both of them—into trouble. The cantina down in Santa Fe, when Immanuel killed the Mexican captain with a single punch, the wife he'd brought back, Flying Feathers, who was still up at their cabins, Uzziah hoped, and they left her without a word, but sincerely, that was more Uzziah's fault than Immanuel's. The trouble they had with the Apache, and if he thought too long about it, he might start to resent the man, and he didn't want that, but he decided he would say something about his drinking which would cut his life short if he weren't careful. They both were at their long poles pushing the raft, sometimes in a circle, but always keeping it in the middle of the Missouri.

"I have somethin' I wanna talk with you about," Uzziah said.

"Well, I can't tell ya how much I enjoy yer beatin' round the bush about it," Immanuel said sarcastically.

"Being that way won't help the discussion."

"Spit it out, will ya, yer like an old woman sometimes."

"Ya drink too much."

"Hell, don't ya think I know that?"

"Ya admit it, then?"

"'Course, I do," Immanuel said, looking at his partner as he was wondering what he was getting at.

"Ya must stop."

"Never!"

"End of discussion?"

"Absolutely."

"Won't ya hear me out?"

"Go ahead, I swear yer like havin' a wife I never married."

"We get into a lot of trouble."

"That's fer sure," Immanuel said.

"And it circles 'round to yer drinkin'!"

"How so?"

Uzziah went through a list of troubles they'd suffered because Immanuel had been drunk at the time. When he finished, he just stood there.

"Well, it's good to know yer not holdin' grudges now, ain't it?"

"But ya refuse to take the responsibility fer those times," Uzziah berated him.

"Okay, but have ya thought 'bout all the fun we'd missed if I hadn't ventured out in my drunkenness?"

"Like gettin' buried alive?" Uzziah asked, his eyebrows shooting up over his eyes.

Immanuel didn't say anything. He fussed with the

long pole, pretended he was having trouble steering with it, got frustrated with that, then said, "Wish I had a drink right now."

"I got whiskey, ifn ya want some."

Immanuel looked at Uzziah, he knew he was lying. If his partner had whiskey, he would know it, and as far as he was concerned, there was none.

"I'm not teasin', partner, really."

"And where is this imaginary hooch?"

"In my saddlebags in the tent."

Immanuel looked at Uzziah, he cocked his head, and licked his lips, then he sat down his pole and dove into the tent. There was a thrashing about, and then—

"Eureka!" Immanuel came crawling from the tent with the pint bottle in his hand.

"Told ya."

"Where did ya get this gift from the gods?"

"At Vrain trading post."

"It ain't been opened," Immanuel said, observing it was still sealed.

"That's a fact."

"Can I?"

"No, we have a nip tonight when we beach," Uzziah said.

"God, ifn ya were a woman, I'd beat ya soundly," he said in exasperation as he started to put the pint in his deerskin coat.

"No, back in me saddle bags ifn ya please."

"Ya bastard, ya no-good, secretive bastard," Immanuel said as he put the pole down once again, and crawled inside the tent, then came back out, "There ya happy now?"

Uzziah put his pole down and the raft began to

circle in the middle of the stream. He walked over to Immanuel, who backed up as far as he could without falling off the raft. Uzziah looked at him, then reached inside his vest and pulled the bottle out.

"Yer a thievin' crook who'd steal the pennies off a dead man's eyes," Uzziah said, and he put the bottle back in the tent, inside his saddlebags.

"I was only worried that ifn we sank, it might be lost," Immanuel whined.

"Lyin' bastard, that's what yer are."

They both went back to their poles and straitened the raft up in the stream.

"Ya got a problem," Uzziah said plainly to his partner.

"Yeah, you!"

———

They beached that night on the southern side of the river. They had been looking for an island, but hadn't found one. Uzziah cooked dinner as usual, and Immanuel hunted. He shot a jackrabbit, and that was it. Along with the bacon and beans, it tasted fine roasted over the fire.

The horses were hobbled with wang leather off the saddles, and Uzziah hoped it would hold. It had on the island, but you never knew? Uzziah brought out the pint from his saddlebags. Immanuel's eyes grew big.

"Yer lookin' at it like it were the Holy Grail," Uzziah said.

"Might as well be, the way you keep hidin' it!"

Uzziah took a nip and passed it to Immanuel. Before he took it, Uzziah spoke, "Just a snort, no more."

"Yes, Mother," Immanuel said and tipped the pint up and actually brought it down rather quickly. "Am I a good boy?"

"The best, old son, the best," Uzziah said, and corking it back up, he placed it back in the saddlebags, and an expression of doom came over Immanuel's face.

"Prick teaser," he muttered under his breath.

"I heard that."

"I should hope so."

They both went to sleep fairly fast, and Uzziah could hear the horses—and Jenny, who wasn't hobbled —eating away at the grasses nearby.

Uzziah thought he was having a dream, he was in the middle of a party, and all these people were laughing and talking, and the piano player was playing some tune he'd heard before, and the lights, my God, the lights were enough to blind you, then he woke up.

Silhouetted by the lights from a paddleboat steamer, Immanuel had the bottle raised to his lips and was chugging on the pint.

"Caught me," he said as he brought the pint down.

"Well, at least we know now they come up this far," Uzziah said.

"We ought to make Fort Manuel with the next few days, we drop the raft and wait fer a paddleboat south to St. Louis."

"I know you'll be happy when we're on the boat," Uzziah said.

"Won't you?"

"Just don't get us into any trouble, okay?"

"Here," Immanuel said as he tossed the bottle to Uzziah, "Sorry 'bout sneaking it from yer bag."

Uzziah took a drink and tossed it back.

"Finish it."

"Really?"

"The sooner it's gone, the better."

————

Immanuel was right, they made Fort Manuel the next night. Uzziah was glad they hadn't pulled in in the middle of the day. It wasn't that he was embarrassed by the Mandan vessel, it was just, well, he was embarrassed by it.

They got the horses off, and Jenny, then the sawbuck went back on the donkey, and she seemed actually glad to have a job. They camped near the fort and would explore the next morning.

They were awakened by reveille, which wasn't exactly what they had been used to. Jenny brayed appreciatively at the bugle sounds, and that had Uzziah and Immanuel laughing before their first cup of coffee, so that was something.

Immanuel went to the fort to check on the paddle-boat schedule south, while Uzziah took care of the horses and Jenny.

"I sold the raft," Immanuel told him when he got back.

"I thought you were gonna send it back to the Mandans?"

"Yeah, nah, dumb, besides these fellas offered me too much to refuse," Immanuel said, showing Uzziah the money he'd gotten for the raft.

"Damn, old son, we're in the wrong business," Uzziah said smiling.

"Nah, stealing is one of the oldest businesses in the

world," Immanuel said and shrugged.

"I still feel bad, maybe we can visit them and pay 'em back."

"Yeah, right after we walk on the moon and shoot the cow that jumps over it!"

"Just an idea," Uzziah said, still feeling foggy about taking the raft and the pelts.

"This will git us rooms, rooms on the boiler deck, and we won't be sleepin' with the horses," Immanuel said.

"And we won't be spendin' it on booze, right?"

"Well," Immanuel said, "we can have a little fun, right?"

———

Two days later, they bought their room on the paddle wheeler. It was cheaper to have one room and not two. Besides, they had slept near each other for the past few years. The horses were glad to get on the main deck, where horses were stalled. They had to pay extra to feed them oats every day, and they were glad to do so.

The first night they wandered through the saloons where they served liquor, you could sit along the railing and watch the water go by, or take a turn in a game of cards. Immanuel was watching one of the card games, and this worried Uzziah. Uzziah was beginning to think that Immanuel was right, he was rather like a wife to the man. He didn't want his partner to gamble away the money he'd gotten from the sale of the giant stolen raft. He knew that they were ill-gotten gains, and here he was going back to see his poor, sick Irish mother. Hell was certainly opening for him! Immanuel saw him watching him, so Uzziah, not wanting to be a stick-in-the-mud, got a drink, whiskey and water, took it out on the deck, and sat in a chair watching the moon reflecting off the Missouri River.

"You look like you could handle yourself anywhere," came a voice from the darkness.

Uzziah looked over and there was a young lady sitting by herself in a darkened corner.

"Well, I can," he said, trying not to brag.

"My husband is stationed up at Fort Mandan and I've just come from a visit," she said as she pulled her chair closer to where he was sitting, so they wouldn't have to yell at one another. There was quite a bit of falderal coming from the gamblers inside the saloon.

"How did you find the fort?"

"Well, I was thinking of coming to live there with him, but he had told me how desolate it was, and he was right."

"So...you didn't stay?"

"No, we had a fight about him being right and me being wrong, and the next thing I knew I was on this paddle wheeler going back to St. Louis."

"You have a house there?"

"My mother does. Well, my parents did, 'til my father was taken from us."

"I am sorry for your loss," Uzziah said. "May I buy you a refreshment?"

She held up a small punch glass, which he hadn't seen before.

"But, thank you. Can I ask you a question?"

"I think you just did."

"Yes, that's right, well, may I ask you another question?"

"That's two in one night, I'm not sure," he joked.

"Are you what they call a mountain man?"

"You mean am I fat?" he joked again. He was glad to have a conversation with a woman he was sure Immanuel wasn't going to marry and take back to the cabins. If Immanuel kept it up, they would soon have to become Mormons.

He thought she blushed before she answered, but it was hard to tell.

"No, but you are a funny man, and funny goes a long way," she said, reaching out and touching his arm. He wasn't sure that that was permitted in polite society, but America was a place where many things were permitted that were not just years before.

"If you were fat, I would have asked if you were a mountain of a man," she said and laughed. She had a deep laugh and it was pleasant to hear. Her face was young and contoured nicely, and when her dark eyes looked at him askance, he felt oddly attracted to her. Well, that was just his imagination. He was easily fifteen years her senior or more.

"I am, in fact, what they call a mountain man, but I'm not sure who they are really."

"You don't sound like a grizzly fighter and Indian killer," she said in a whisper.

There were great shouts from the saloon, and men's voices were intermingled with the gladness of victory and the grunts of defeat. Uzziah looked over his shoulder and there were stacks of chips in front of Immanuel's place at the table. Well, at least he was winning.

"I take it that's your partner?" she asked.

"Yes, that's Immanuel James Jones."

"I love that name."

"Please don't tell him that," Uzziah said, taking a sip of the bonded whiskey. He had forgotten what it was like to sit and talk with a lady, well, maybe she was, and maybe she wasn't. He wasn't born yesterday, and realized this may all be leading up to something untoward on her part. Not that she was a soiled dove or anything like that, but in these situations, there were often men sitting elsewhere who trained and managed these *girls*. Well, he hadn't felt this comfortable and civilized since he had been back in Virginia in the Shenandoah Valley, and he would play along, what could be the harm?

"Do you gamble?" she asked him. Now, she was getting sort of personal, and he was worried that the conversation was becoming a little less civilized.

"Life's a gamble, isn't it?"

She laughed. "So, you're a philosopher, then?"

"What was it the bard said, 'Life's a stage and we all the actors on it,' or something like that."

"And you know the Lion in the Road?"

"I've never heard him called that!"

"Well, I write a bit. In fact, my papa had a newspaper in St. Louis, and Mama still runs it to this day. Once in a while I send in something, a letter to the editor, you know. She, not the editor, have no idea that it was me, since I use a typewriter that my papa had. Several of the pieces have been published."

"You don't use your real name, then?"

"Heaven to Betsy, no!"

"Might I inquire as to the *nom de plume* you do use?"

"And now, this mountain man is speaking French!"

"Many of the trappers and traders in the mountains, the Rockies are French, you know."

"I'd heard that, but didn't believe it."

"Well, you'd better," Uzziah said, sipping the whiskey and it was almost gone. "Can I get you something else?"

"Yes, a white wine, please," she said, handing him the small punch cup.

He walked into the saloon and Immanuel smiled greatly at him as if he was having the most delirious time of his life. The chips were stacked in front of him, and he didn't seem drunk, and Uzziah supposed he wasn't. He looked back to where he could, in the shaft of light which fell from the saloon, seeing the woman, the young girl he'd been talking with. She smiled at him, and he continued to the bar.

When he came back, he handed her the wine, and he settled into his chair with his whiskey, and looked back onto the waters where the moon was dancing lively.

"It's beautiful, isn't it?" she asked.

"Yes, very. I see the moon all the time where we live, but somehow, it seems more unreal here, reflecting off the river, undulating as it is."

"Yes, yes, I know what you mean," she said and took a sip of wine.

Uzziah wondered where this could all be leading.

"This is very forward of me, and really, Mama will be so upset, but I'd like to talk more with you later. Do you suppose you and Immanuel, by the way, what's your name?"

"I'm Uzziah Ferguson O'Bannon," he said, and then realized that he actually told this woman who lived in St. Louis and was probably familiar with the undersheriff going missing, he'd actually told her his real name, and the name of his partner in crime. He must have looked oddly at her, and she at him.

"Really, that's your name, Uzziah Ferguson O'Bannon?"

"Yes, yes, it is," he admitted, but wished he hadn't.

"Well," she said, "my name is Kate Warne, and I work for Allan Pinkerton, and you, Uzziah Ferguson O'Bannon, are under arrest for the murder of the Pinkerton Agent Robert Spells." She brought from her reticule a .45-caliber derringer and pointed it at his heart.

Uzziah felt the fool, but the enlivened conversation had almost been worth it. What she didn't know was that he and Immanuel had always had a special word which could be shouted at any moment, and it, that word, would tell the other that things had gotten out of hand, and danger was more than imminent, and all bets were off, so to speak.

"Flummadiddle!" Uzziah screamed at the top of his voice.

———

In the saloon, Immanuel heard their danger word, grabbed his earnings off the table, ran the opposite way from where Uzziah was sitting, and dove off the boiler deck. He managed to secure the cash funds which he had acquired before hitting the cold waters of the Missouri and going underwater. With the moonlight shining through the water, he could see the bullets that streaked through at him, fortunately missing, as their trajectories brought bubbles with them. He swam toward the boat not away as some would have thought, and when he'd come under the boat, went deep to avoid the paddle wheel, then grabbed the wheel and, lifting his foot onto it, he rode it to the hurricane deck where, dripping wet, he clung to the facing which barely gave him enough finger hold to secure his position. He could hear the hubbub on the boiler deck as men were shouting and whatever was happening to Uzziah was happening. Well, he thought as he clung there like a fly on the wall, at least this time, it wasn't he who had plunged them into trouble, whatever trouble it was.

4

The night was young, as they once said, and Immanuel made his way up onto the hurricane deck, and once there, crouched in the moonlight, he waited to be discovered. But from what he could hear from the pilot house, a man had been arrested for the suspected murder of an undersheriff in St. Louis and the murder of a Pinkerton Agent in the Rocky Mountains. He guessed that meant they had found the frozen body of Robert Spells. They hadn't really killed him. Robert's own knowledge of the mountains, which could have fit inside a thimble and left room for his thumb, had, in the end, done him in. They had released the man, who obviously had no sense of direction, and he had frozen to death. Perhaps the Catholics would call that a sin of omission on their part.

The general commotion really wasn't as much about the fact that Uzziah Ferguson O'Bannon would finally be brought to justice, but the fact that a woman, one Miss Kate Warne, a young woman highly intelligent and respected so well by Mr. Pinkerton that he had sent her on this special mission to find the murderers of his agent.

Immanuel had no idea just how she had tracked them, but like some Apache native, she had, and by golly, she had found them. He was lucky, if you could call it that, not to be in irons as Uzziah, and he wasn't about to let his friend stay that way.

Obviously, it would be best to get Uzziah away from her clutches before they got to St. Louis, but how? He wished he had a confederate who could help him in his scheme. But first things first. He would have to get dry clothes and alter his appearance as much as possible. The man he had been rivaled with in the card game, the man who had lost the majority of this money to Immanuel was one Quincy Tilman, an English Earl who had come to America to shoot a grizzly bear, and with the help of some expert Injun guides had done just that. During the conversation of play, he had told Immanuel that the skin of the great bear was below, very close to the boiler room, in hopes of keeping it dry and secure. The man was just about the same size as Immanuel, a bit heavier, but pillows could work that magic. He had mentioned that his estate room, he had called it that, was number 5 just down from the saloon. Immanuel would have to wait, and not be discovered, and then he would work his scheme.

Later that night, as the passengers slept and Uzziah was God knows where, Immanuel went down on the boiler deck to room #5. He worked his Bowie knife into the mechanism and popped the lock rather easily.

Quincy Tillman, the Earl of Dead Grizzly, was sound asleep. And like most of us, had his mouth open and his hair was a fright. In fact, most of it was situated on a stand near his bed. The Earl of Dead Grizzly was actually mostly bald! When Immanuel placed his hand over the man's mouth and the knife to his throat, he surrendered like a mouse. Too bad the grizzly hadn't had a knife! The earl was tied up and gagged. When he saw the poor man sitting there his crouch wet from his own piss, he felt sorry for him, and placed the rug back on his head. It didn't seem to fit right, but what the hell! He had other, more important things to do besides rearrange an earl's wig.

Immanuel set to shaving off his great beard and leaving only his gorgeous mustache, which handle barred out past his cheeks. He went through the earl's things and found a wonderful hunting outfit complete with jodhpurs, Wellington riding boots, and a frilly shirt and waistcoat. My God, Immanuel almost fell in love with himself when he looked in the full-length mirror on the door. My, he was one handsome chap. The outfit was completed by a brace of Spies 38 calibers in suspender holsters holding two such percussion pistols. His plan was not fully formed in his mind as he sat opposite the earl, who was now snoring, well, at least he had accepted this particular fate.

———

Uzziah had been tied to one of the chairs in Kate Warne's stateroom. It was the largest of the rooms on the paddle wheeler and had been reserved originally for some earl, who had to take a smaller room, much to his displeasure.

Kate sat in a chair opposite Uzziah, and a man,

well-armed, stood close by. He too, Uzziah thought, must be an agent.

"The man who was gambling, that was Immanuel James Jones, wasn't it?" Kate asked, blowing smoke from a ready-made small cigar.

"I don't know," Uzziah said, wondering what had happened to Immanuel once he'd jumped ship. He certainly hoped he got away, but there were so many shots delivered into the water after him that he doubted that his partner was still alive.

"Well, we're backing up and turning about. I'd like to either find his bullet-riddled body or perhaps his drowned body, but in either case, I'd like to know, wouldn't you?" she asked. She could see that he was interested in her small cigar. "Would you like to try it?"

"Wouldn't mind," Uzziah said, "but ya'd have to untie my hands."

"Ridiculous," she said, and she stood up, walked the two steps to where he was bound, and offered a drag from the one she was smoking.

Uzziah opened his mouth and thought about biting her when she offered the small cigar, but what would that get him but a blow from the young, strong gentleman standing in the same suite of rooms.

She placed it near enough to his lips that, stretching forward, he was able to take a drag, then French inhaled it through his nose, and as he expelled the smoke, made a nice smoke ring.

"Oh, I wish I could do that," she said, obviously admiring the ring as it made its way lazily across the room. The man with her stuck his finger in it, and it was destroyed.

"What'd you do that for?" she asked him, annoyed.

"Don't know, just felt like it," he said, looking at her.

"Well, don't do anything, and I do mean anything, unless you ask me first. Do you understand?"

He hesitated too long and she asked the question again, this time with a bit more force. "Do you understand!?!"

"Yes, ma'am," he said apologetically.

"And don't call me, ma'am, that infuriates me even more than doing things which you haven't asked my permission to do. Do you understand that?"

"Yes, ma—" he almost said it again, and she glared at him. Uzziah liked this woman in spite of the fact that she had, in effect, ensnared him. She had done so without seeming to be anything but a woman, but when he thought back, he remembered thinking that she might be a fancy whore, and that there must have been a man close by. He wasn't wrong, this other Pinkerton agent was close by, and he had emptied both his guns at Immanuel as he leaped from the paddle wheeler and fired even more shots from his rifle into the water in hopes of killing him. She was rather enjoying the manner in which she was treating him, well, he had to be her inferior, or she wouldn't be talking to him about that, yes?

"You want information from me, am I correct?"

She looked back at Uzziah and smiled. She had an honest and quite lovely face, and he was glad to have removed the annoyance of the underling she had to deal with.

"That's right, I do."

"Tell ya what, ya reveal some of how this particular capture came 'bout, and I'll answer yer questions, deal?"

She was glad to have gotten him into the position of bargaining, that was usually a good sign, in her book. Once a prisoner began to bargain, it wasn't long before they revealed all sorts of information.

"Yes, okay, I'll even let you ask the first question, how's that?"

"Kate, I mean Miss Warne, I don't believe Allan would want you to go this route," the younger agent said.

"Just a minute, Mr. O'Bannon, while I deal with this nagging problem."

"You bet," Uzziah said.

"In the first place, *Tom*, if Mr. Pinkerton were here, I'm sure that he wouldn't want you to call him by his first name. Are you, in fact, on a first-name basis with the founder of the Pinkerton Agency?"

"No ma'am," he said and immediately regretted it.

"You are, in fact, a brainless ninny, aren't you, *Tom*?" She accented his name every time she said it, and for some reason, that was making the young man irritated.

He didn't answer, so she continued.

"I really don't give a flying fart whether you believe Mr. Pinkerton would want me to go this, as you put it, *route*, or not. Mr. Pinkerton is sitting back in Chicago, enjoying one of his big, fat cigars, and he hasn't thought of you since the last time you were in his office. Oh, wait a minute, you've never been in his office, have you, *Tom*?"

"Ah...no, ma—I mean, simply, no, I haven't."

"And do you know why that is, *Tom*?"

"I think I do."

"Well, don't bother me with your inane answer

because it doesn't match mine. You haven't been in his office because you are a junior, junior, junior member of the Agency, and to tell the truth, you were only allowed along because I thought I might need some muscle. You do have muscles, don't you, *Tom*?"

"Yes." At least he hadn't said ma'am that time.

"And I suppose you have so many of those afore-mentioned muscles that some of them are between your ears, right, *Tom*?"

All Uzziah could think was that he was certainly glad he wasn't *Tom*. She was a hellcat, and now, her cattery nature was being expelled upon this Tom, and whatever Tom got was something which Uzziah could avoid. Good for her.

Now, Tom was simply agreeing with her by shaking his head up and down.

"Good use of your neck muscles, *Tom*, really fine work. Now, go to the saloon and have a soda or something, I really don't care."

"But—"

She stood and pulled out the double-barreled derringer that she had pulled on Uzziah, and Tom fully expected it to be fired into his midsection.

Tom left in a hurry.

She turned and looked at Uzziah.

"It's so hard to find good help these days," she said, then continued, "Where were we?"

"I was about to ask you my first quandary?"

"Yes, of course, shoot."

"How'd ya find us?"

"Well, the answer to that would take all day, because it's taken six months of looking to simply see you. Suffice it to say that we found Mr. Robert Spells when the spring thaw came, and you really should have taken his notebook from him. He made meticulous notes. And I realize he died a natural death by freezing in the Rockies, but think somehow that you and Mr. Jones had something to do with that freezing."

"The man had no sense, or use, of direction," Uzziah confessed.

"I knew that, and I had advised Mr. Pinkerton against it, but the young buck was so willing, so very willing."

"He was that."

"Glad we can agree on that. So, within the afore-mentioned notebook, he wasn't specific, but there were enough notes that I got a feel for the both of you. Especially you, I think he liked you."

"Well, I did keep Immanuel from killin' him outright."

"You see, I was right, he did like you."

"And lookie here," she said as she took a weathered leather notebook from the top of the desk in the suite. Opening it, where there was a paper marker, she held it in front of him. There, on paper, drawn rather expertly was a sketch of Uzziah Ferguson O'Bannon in pencil. Uzziah had an artist friend back in the Shenandoah Valley who couldn't draw that well, and Robert Spells had done all this from memory, extraordinary!

"For what it's worth, I liked him."

"Did you, really? Well, letting him freeze to death all by himself was certainly proof of that, wasn't it?"

"Yep."

"You Westerners have certainly made shorthand of the English language, haven't you?"

Uzziah nodded his head in agreement.

"Oh, don't do that, it reminds me of the one who just left. Is it my turn?"

"Believe it is."

"Where were you going and why?"

"Immanuel and I?"

"Yes."

"St. Louis to sell our pelts."

"The silk hat industry, right?"

"Yep."

"So, beaver no longer bringing an affordable, shall we say, revenue for its pelts has driven you east, correct?"

"Right."

"I believe it's your turn now," she said and lit another one of her short, thin cigars.

———

Immanuel had finally come up with the shadings of a plan, and he felt that any more sitting around thinking wasn't going to bring about the filling-in of that plan, since so much depended on its quick execution. He patted the earl on the head, he was awake now, and flinched badly when he was patted, plus the wig fell off. Immanuel just looked at him and shook his head.

"Trust me, Sir Earl, ya look better without the peri-wig, really."

The earl looked at Immanuel strangely, and from that day forward, he never wore the toupee again. Sometimes, adversaries have the best advice.

"Try not to wait up," he said to the Earl of Grizzly Death, and the earl tried to speak without making any sense in the least bit. He wanted to thank Immanuel for the best story he could tell when he got back to jolly ole England, even better than the grizzly that he had shot at, but missed. Thank God, the Native American guide had been along!

Having taken the key to the room from the earl, he locked it. He may, if the plan succeeded at all, have use for the room again.

Immanuel roamed the decks and the two saloons. He ran across one of the men he'd won money from and they tipped their hats to each other, but he, Immanuel, wasn't recognized. That was a good test, since when one losses vast sums to someone in a card game, and he *had* cheated, how else could he have won all those hands, you have a tendency to recognize the man who has bilked you out of your funds.

Going into the second saloon, he saw the young buck who had fired at him at really close range and missed. He'd taken the man's inability to shoot straight into this plan, and he was ever so glad that he was still wandering the ship. He did not see any other law person on the ship. That too, was taken into his plan. They had turned the vessel around and were using a lot of wood to go back upstream, he guessed, in an effort to discover his body, if, in fact, he had been killed. Now, all he needed to do was watch the only law on the ship, and he would inevitably take him to the room where his partner was being held.

"May I have a beer?" he asked in what he thought might be the semblance of a British accent.

The barkeep looked at him oddly, then poured the beer, put it on the bar in front of Immanuel, and went to serve someone else. He would have to keep his conversation to a minimum, that was a fact. Unfortunately, the man whom he had discovered to be the only visible law on the boat approached him and sat down on the stool next to him. *Good God!* Immanuel thought.

"You with the other Brit?" the man asked him.

"Hmm," Immanuel grunted, and took a quick drink of beer to fill his mouth with something besides fake English-accented words.

"He lost a great deal to one of the pirates who was onboard."

So, thought Immanuel, now they were pirates, he guessed the law dog made that assumption since they were on board a vessel on water. How astute.

"I fired enough shots at him, the one who jumped. He's probably dead, don't ya think?"

"Probably," Immanuel said in the bass voice of a Brit.

"I like yer accent," the law dog said.

"Hmm," Immanuel said, drinking more beer. He hoped he didn't have to sit like this for long or he would be tipsy from too much beer.

"Well, I gots to get back to work," the law dog said reluctantly. He didn't say it reluctantly, but you could tell he wanted to sit and drink, but duty called.

"Avoir," Immanuel said with a sort of French accent that was probably a mistake, but it was done.

"You Brits talk all kinda languages, don't ya, and with the correct inflections, I admire that," the law dog said as he left the saloon.

Immanuel waited the appropriate amount of time and followed him to the suite where he knocked on the door, three shots, two long, and it was opened by a woman. The same woman who had taken Uzziah prisoner. Now that he knew where Uzziah was, he would take care of the other part of the plan.

He took the stairs to the main deck and overheard a sailor talking to the captain of the vessel.

"Sir, we searched both the shore and the water, we ain't seen no bodies. But we're growing short on wood, we'll have to go ashore before the wood station."

"Very well, tell the pilot to turn us back on course, and I will inform Miss Warne."

So, that was the name of the woman who had taken Uzziah prisoner. He hoped she wasn't beating the crap out of him while he was impersonating someone from across the pond.

On the main deck, he wandered down to the stock area. There was a man seated there, probably the one in charge of seeing that they were fed and watered.

"Can I helps ya, sira?" the Black man asked.

"No, no, just checking on the horses."

"Ya gots to see this cheer jackass," the man said incorrectly, since he knew, he was referring to Jenny.

"Really, what is that?"

"Damnest thing I ever did see, sira, the horse gots the cross of Jesus on his back," the old Black man said as he led him back into the stalls. Sure enough, there was Jenny, and he knew she would recognize him, not because he looked the same but because he smelled the same. Unfortunately, he'd have to tie this man up for the plan to succeed.

Sure enough, Jenny started braying when he stood opposite her stall.

"She likes ya, sira," the man said as Immanuel hit the poor man over the head with one of the brace of pistols, but not too hard. He then took some rope hanging there and tied him up, and gagged him also. If he didn't hurry, there wouldn't be anybody who wasn't tied up and gagged.

He put the sawbuck saddle back on Jenny, and the pelts, they were heavy, but they had been separated into manageable piles. They were back in the sawbuck and she was braying again, but no one up top could possibly have heard her over the engines.

Shadow and his horse, he'd have to name the horse eventually, but it seemed any time he did something like that, the horse was shot, drowned, or killed in some way. He got both horses saddled and ready to go. He was a bit worried about Jenny swimming with the pelts on her back, but who knew, really?

5

When the door to the suite in which Pinkerton Agents—Kate Warne and Tom, the junior agent—had Uzziah tied to a chair burst open, Immanuel was rewarded by his judgment of the junior agent's marksmanship by two shots which went both wide of their mark—one on the right side of him, and the other on the left. He clobbered the junior agent with the butt of his pistol and he went down, then knocked the derringer from the hand of the not really bad looking woman, and grabbed her at the mouth to keep her from screaming. She struggled in his arms and he liked her muscles and fustiness. In a different situation, he would have been lunging into her as she writhed about.

Uzziah was looking at this stranger who had done these things and wondered why anyone who did not know him was bothering to do such things. Then Immanuel spoke as he tossed a Bowie knife to Uzziah, who took it with both hands and cut the ropes on his feet.

"Get yerself undone," Immanuel said.

"What happened to yer face?" Uzziah said as he cut his hands free, and stood up trying to get the feeling back in his feet, he danced around a bit.

"You are happy to see me, even dancing happy!"

"Again, what happened to Herbert?" Immanuel had named his beard in a state of boredom one winter and it had stuck.

"Herbert committed seppuku, otherwise known as ritual disembowelment, by a very sharp razor," Immanuel said as he took the ropes which Uzziah had cut and wrapped them around the wrists of the woman.

"You are too smart to keep living this life of crime, Mr. Jones," she said, looking him right in the eyes.

"And you, my dear, are too energetic to be wasting your time and energy on chasing free men!"

"You actually knew what seppuku is? My God, what you—" Her speech to get Immanuel to turn himself in was cut short by a bandana which was stuffed way back into her mouth until her eyes bulged.

"I know it feels as if you will suffocate, but it's only happened to one person I've done this to, and she was a weak soul," Immanuel said, and Miss Warne's eyes kept bulging. Then he bound her feet.

There was running on the deck as some of the crew were running around trying to find out where the shots came from.

"We gots to hurry, O'Bannon," he said.

They stepped out onto the passageway and Immanuel grabbed a member of the crew who ran by. "Tell the captain to dock immediately, we're nearly out of fuel," Immanuel said, trying to sound official. That really wasn't part of his plan, but it might work.

The crew member thought who knows what, but he ran off.

On their way to the main deck and the horses, the paddlewheel actually started toward the shore. Would wonders never cease?

The horses were right where he'd left them, and throwing out the stock gangplank, the two men, followed by Jenny—when did she not follow—rode up to where the gangplank rubbed against the side of the shore.

Shadow jumped to the shore and Uzziah managed to keep his seat, and Immanuel's horse took the gangplank, and so did Jenny.

The good news was that the air horn of the paddle wheeler screamed into the night, and several shots from somebody's rifle missed them, barely. Uzziah thought it was probably Kate who had used the rifle, and Immanuel had to agree, but how the hell did she get loose? Maybe she had been an escape artist in a circus, once?

They rode the river faster than the paddle wheeler could possibly have traveled.

"We got to let these horses rest," Uzziah said, then he looked back. "Plus all the money we got in the world is somewhere back there with Jenny."

They pulled into a set of trees that were far enough away from the paddle wheeler that the smoke from its smokestacks was barely visible.

"Were there any more horses down in the stable area?" Uzziah asked.

"No, matter of fact, there weren't. I hope I didn't clobber that old nigger too hard on the noggin."

"He was moanin' when we were gettin' saddled up," Uzziah said.

"Good, means he weren't dead. We gotta take care of the paddle wheeler, partner," Immanuel said.

"Sink it?!?"

"Nah," Immanuel said, but did not elaborate.

"Good, here comes Jenny."

"She looks wore out, pard. Say what'd ya think of that miraculous escape?"

"We're not even, yet," Uzziah said, grinning.

"You old bastard. Who woulda guessed that woman was an agent, huh?"

"Yeah, remind me to tell ya about what she told me, but let's get situated about fifty yards from the river, where nobody'll be able to come back at us," Uzziah said.

They rode, not quite as fast, for about another half hour, the smoke from the paddle boat was getting closer. They could just see it in the moonlight. They found a few hills and sat up there with the stock out of sight, just in case anybody did have a long-range rifle. Uzziah laid down on the ridge of the furthest hill, and Immanuel, thinking ahead, went down a bit and sat himself up.

Fairly soon, the *Merry Chase*—that was actually the name of the vessel, Uzziah couldn't believe it, thought he should have taken note of that before they got on her —was closing in.

"We're gonna take out the stern wheel mechanics, the center there where the thing fits in and is able to turn with no effort," Immanuel yelled to his partner.

"Gotcha!"

"If we're lucky, they won't be able to see what we're

foalin' 'til it's broke and the boiler is pushin' hard, but unable to make headway."

———

Kate Warne and Tom were sitting at the bar in the first saloon and having a drink. It looked from the redness of his ears that Tom had been taking a few earfuls and was suffering from it. She was in a brooding mood.

"We had them sons a bitches, we had them!"

"Yes, ma'am, we did," Tom said, and she turned and looked at him like she might shoot him.

"Sorry."

"Sorry shot, sorry partner, sorry at feeding the kitty, what else are you sorry at, huh?"

Tom had never heard a woman, any woman but a whore use that kind of language, he turned red with embarrassment.

"You should be very embarrassed, but not at my colorful use of the English language, but at your marksmanship, if you can call it that!? How could you miss a man who was no more than five feet from you? How!?!"

"He got the drop on me."

"Next time I go out with anyone, they are going to go to the range and show me their marksmanship, that's a fact. I don't care how well hung they are!"

The other gentlemen at the saloon were having a time listening to this hellcat, and they were just glad that they weren't Tom.

There was a sound like distant thunder and Kate Warne looked around. "Did you hear that?"

"What?"

"Nothing," she said, then nearly the same sound

came again. She ran out on the deck that surrounded the boiler deck and looked up at the sky, "There are clouds way over there, but we couldn't possibly hear thunder from there, could we?"

There was a splintering sound from the back of the boat, and both Kate and Tom looked, and pieces of wood close to the center of the wheel came flying off, then the thunder sound, two of them close together.

"Them son a bitches are destroying the wheel mechanism," she said as she ran up the stairs to the roof bell and she began to ring it incessantly. Tom covered his ears, she was making such a racket.

The pilot came running down from the pilot house, "What are you doing, Madam?"

"They are destroying the wheel mechanisms!" she shouted to him.

Immediately, he ran to the stern of the Texas deck and looked down at the wheel. Two more closely coordinated 50-caliber slugs tore at the mechanism, and that was the last straw. The mechanism that held the ball bearings broke, the wheel drooped sideways, and the pressure from the engine room kept turning the wheel, which caused it to catch and start breaking apart. The pilot ran to the pilot house, and even back at the stern, Kate Warne could hear him shouting down to the engine room to disengage the wheel, but it was too late. It ground and ground, then groaning, it smashed the wheel against the struts which held it in place, completely destroying the wheel, the boat listed in the water and began to turn sideways in the Missouri.

Another shot clipped the mast that held up the American flag, and it toppled sideways into the river and disappeared.

"What just happened?" Tom asked.

Kate Warne looked at her junior Pinkerton Agent and shook her head.

"They just stopped us in our tracks, and signaled our surrender by taking down our flag! They'll be in St. Louis before we make it halfway there."

"We must notify the sheriff there!" Tom yelled.

"Got any homing pigeons on you?" she asked, then added, "I'm going to get drunk, then we're going back to the room, where I hope you will surely improve your no-pants dancing."

———

Uzziah and Immanuel were jumping up and down and screaming. Jenny thought she'd done something wrong and ran off.

"Don't worry, she'll be back," Uzziah said.

"Yeah," Immanuel said, watching her run off. He rubbed his naked chin, and Uzziah looked at him. "Don't say a damned word!"

"No, no, you've given me an idea," Uzziah said.

———

They rode for the rest of the day, and the smoke from the paddle wheel completely disappeared from the horizon.

Uzziah made a special supper for Immanuel, after all, he had shaved off a good six years' growth of his beard for him. Immanuel came back with a baby buffalo, and they cooked and ate the hump and tongue first. Uzziah gave his pard the majority of that, after all, he had made the shot. Then they had tender baby buffalo steaks.

The next morning, Uzziah got up early and prepared a surprise for Immanuel.

When Immanuel James Jones rolled out of his bedroll, there was a man standing there with a pistol pointed at him.

"You're under arrest and have been captured by the Pinkerton Agency. Don't make any sudden moves or I'll shoot yer nades off," the man said.

"Uzziah?" Immanuel said, rubbing his head. "Please tell me it's you."

"It is," Uzziah said, and started laughing.

"This is yer plan, eh?"

"They won't recognize either one of us in St. Louis!" Uzziah said.

6

The two gentlemen who walked down the boardwalk, headed for The Growling Catfish, looked like they might be two men in search of the other side of the tracks. When they entered the bar, the owner, Charlie Watts, treated them with a great deal of respect, until Uzziah spoke.

"Charlie, yer brown nosin' is gettin' better," Uzziah said.

He turned and looked at the big man, and looking closer, he started laughing. "You big bear, I shoulda known it was you, and that there is yer friend." As he started to say his name, Uzziah put his index finger to Charlie's lips.

"So, what are you two up to now?"

"We're goin' to Virginny, my ma's been taken sick."

"Well, don't expect yer family to know who the hell you are," the owner said. "Drinks are on the house and so are the pokes."

"Very generous, my friend," Immanuel said, "but

we're on the train in a couple of hours, we just wanted to see an old friend."

They had a drink and told stories of their cabins in the Rockies and several of the soiled doves offered free pokes, what the hell?

"I didn't want to spoil the reunion back there, but what's this about ole Virginny?"

"Take a look at this," Uzziah said, handing him the missive from his ma.

Immanuel read as they walked along, whistled at one point, then handed the letter back to Uzziah.

"So, we partners, no?"

"Yeah, a'course," Uzziah said, wondering where Immanuel was going with this.

"Ya coulda told me about this a lot earlier."

"I was afraid ya wouldn't go along with me."

"And miss the cooking ya been talkin' 'bout for this past many years, are ya kiddin' me?!?"

"So, you'll go?"

"Wouldn't miss it fer the world, Uzziah, not fer the world," Immanuel said and put his arm around his partner as they walked down the boardwalk toward the train station.

———

When they boarded the eastbound train for Clarksburg, Virginia, on the Baltimore and Ohio railroad, they took seats across from each other so that it would be easier for them to talk. Sit next to a man on a train and try talking to him, and you've got a pinched nerve in your neck.

The train was filling up fast, and both mountain

men, both disguised as, well, they couldn't make up their minds what they looked like, they'd just wait and see how people would treat them. Their leather satchels with everything in them were stashed up top, and even their Hawkens, they'd bought two really nice leather cases for them, and they looked like brand-new rifles. Shadow and Immanuel's horse were in the stock car, and fed, and all was right with the world. They had left Jenny at a hostler and given the man enough to keep her for a year. She brayed the entire time they were within earshot.

"Is this seat taken?" a sweating, balding salesman, with his bowler in his hand and carrying a sampler's case, asked Immanuel.

"It sure is, we's both waiting on our wives to get onboard," Immanuel said, pointing to Uzziah.

"I see, sorry, but I think yer pullin' my leg, so, ifn ya don't mind, I'll sit next to the other gentleman," the salesman said, and Uzziah moved over a bit, after all, he was a big man, the salesman, that is.

"Here they come now," Immanuel said, smiling.

The sweating salesman turned and looked.

Uzziah turned and two—well, what looked like saloon girls—dressed way too much to be traveling on the train, were struggling with their bags as they made their way down the aisle. Everybody who had a vacant seat either covered it with a bag or looked away when they asked about the seats. It was plain and simple, soiled dove discrimination.

Immanuel got up and walked down the aisle, Uzziah could hear him without turning around.

"Here, we thought y'all was never gonna come. Did ya have trouble at the livery?"

The youngest and prettiest of them took Immanuel's cue.

"Yes, darlin', we did, never thought we'd get here in time." She smiled big as Immanuel smiled back, taking her bags. The older soiled dove, by no means ancient and looking just a little short of the younger one, smiled, too, but Immanuel only had so many hands.

"Uzziah, are ya gonna make yer wife carry her bags, get over chere boy, and help the poor woman out, she looks exhausted."

Uzziah got up and came back, squeezing by Immanuel and the pretty one, and smiling, he took the bags from the older one.

"Sorry, dear, I was daydreamin'."

"As ya have a tendency to do," she said, scolding him, and Uzziah nearly started laughing as he came down the aisle behind her.

The salesman stood there gawking.

"Do ya mind gettin' out of the way for our women-folk?"

"No, no, no, sorry, thought ya was chaffing me," he said, then to the pretty one he bowed slightly, and picking up his sample case, walked off.

Immanuel's wife was about five foot six tall with dyed blond hair that was piled up on her head in a chignon, curls dangling down beside her lovely oval-shaped head. Her nose was small and pretty, and she had cheeks rouged to perfection with blue eyes accenting her cheeks. When she smiled the cutest dimples appeared on either side of her perfect cupid's bow mouth covered in what Immanuel would have called, whore red. She sat by the window and smiled up at Immanuel as he put her bags up alongside his Hawken.

The other soiled dove sat across from her friend. She was shorter, about five foot two with green eyes and auburn hair. There were crow's feet beside each green eye, and when she smiled, the feet were accentuated as they were at this very instance. Her hair was left long and draped over her shoulders, and her mouth was sensuous without being pouty.

Uzziah slung her bags up by his Hawken as if they weighed nothing and sat down beside her.

Everyone was smiling back and forth 'til all the attention that they had gathered from the other passengers subsided.

"You two are a Godsend," the blonde whispered, "I'm Gloria, and this is my friend is Cassandra."

"Allow me to introduce both of us?" he asked, looking at Uzziah, who nodded graciously.

"I go by the moniker, Immanuel James Jones, and across from me is my partner in crime, Uzziah Ferguson O'Bannon," he said, and both men took off their Stetsons, which were as new as the morning dew.

"Well," Gloria said, "it's been a long time since we came across such well-dressed and gracious gentlemen."

"What part of the valley are ya from?" Uzziah asked.

"Would that valley be the Delta of Venus?" Gloria asked him.

Uzziah blushed. "No, ma'am, that would be the Shenandoah Valley."

"Oh, goodness," Gloria said, putting her hand to her chest and seeming really embarrassed. "I am sorry, yes, well, as you probably guessed, I am from Thornton Gap," she said, smiling. "And you?"

"Front Royal," Uzziah said.

"Oh, I was at the Skyline Caverns when I was a girl."

"They're wonderful, aren't they?" Uzziah asked.

"Well, my papa took me there, and once underground, I began to have the most uncomfortable feelings. I couldn't breathe, I just couldn't. My papa said to quit actin' crazy, but I simply couldn't breathe. I'm 'fraid I embarrassed him very much. He had to carry me, and I was nearly ten years old, up the shaft to the outside—all the time I was crying until I saw the clouds and the blue sky."

"You're simply scared of small spaces, my dear, you probably don't care for small rooms, and closed-in places neither?" Immanuel asked, then added, "I had a squaw wife who would not enter a cave, even if there was a million dollars lying there. She said, her medicine man had told her that she remembered too well being in the body of her mother, and goin' into any small space, reminded her of that."

Uzziah looked at Gloria and Cassandra, who were hiding smiles behind their hands.

"They think yer full of hooey," Uzziah said, and the two soiled doves began laughing openly.

"We're sorry, we really are, but mountain men come up with the strangest stories," Gloria said.

"How'd ya know we's mountain folk?" Immanuel asked, not really insulted.

"Well, for one thing, yer all white around yer throat and face. Ya portably just shaved, right?"

"That's a fact," Uzziah said and smiled at Gloria.

"Maybe Gloria should be yer wife?" Immanuel said.

"Look, boys," Cassandra joined in whispering, "Ya have both of us fer a price, right?"

Immanuel smiled and leaned in close to Cassandra.

"We ain't rich, ya know?"

"Begging ain't manly, so don't go there," Cassandra said.

Uzziah started laughing like there was no tomorrow, which got both the girls laying, he did have an infectious laugh.

"How 'bout the livestock car at the next water stop?" Immanuel asked.

"Mountain man, you can ride me just like yer stock ifn ya got the money," Gloria said.

Immanuel stopped the conductor who was walking past.

"When's the next water stop?"

"Right before we enter the mountains, sir."

"And when's that?"

"Couple of days," the conductor said and walked on by.

"We can use the hopper ifn that's too long to wait," Cassandra said, then added, "It's at the end of the car."

"Ain't it kinda small?" Immanuel asked.

"Ya know it ain't the size of the ship, it's the motion of the ocean," Cassandra said, and both soiled doves laughed.

"I meant the hopper, ain't much room in there, is there?"

"Ifn ya don't mind seeing the other one doin' the other one, there's plenty of room," Gloria said.

"Well, hell, what we waitin' fer?" Uzziah asked.

First, Uzziah and Cassandra went down and went into the hopper, which was essentially a hole in the floor, then Immanuel and Gloria went in.

It was a tight squeeze, but the men sat down, the ladies got them going, then they sat on the men. Everything was going fine, when there were screams, and a man's voice.

"All right, take out everythin' I do mean eveythin' which is of value, and my partner here will be by to collect those precious valuables. Ifn ya hold back y'all be shot, simple as that!" the voice admonished them.

In the car they were in, which was the last before the caboose, one man held everybody still with his six-shooter, and the other fellow, probably his brother, much younger, and most likely his first train holdup, went down the line, holding his hat out for everyone to drop goodies into it. Both the men on the train had masks on.

"Earl, I do believe this man's a cheatin' us," the boy said to the bigger man with the gun.

"Don't use my name, ya fool!" Earl said as he made his way down to where his brother, held out his hat. "Any y'all move, yer dead!" the man with the gun reminded them.

"What seems to be the trouble?" he asked his brother.

"Lookie that there chronometer," the younger man pointed to the gold chain which hung from the man's vest.

"Give it over!" Earl said.

"I will not—" the man began, then BOOM!

"Ya kilt him, Earl, ya kilt him," the kid said as smoke roiled from the hole in the dead man's vest and screams came from the passengers.

"I told ya not to use my name, now the spot's comin' up where the horses'll be, grab the watch off the stiff and let's get rollin'!" Earl commanded.

The door to the hopper came open nice and slow. Immanuel had both Spies 38s from his suspender holsters and Uzziah had his Bowie knife out. Smartly, the women had stayed in the hopper.

"Earl, there's trouble," the younger brother said, and he pointed behind his brother.

Earl turned fast, but before he could get a shot off, both Spies 38s resounded in the train car.

Earl looked down at his vest.

"My vest's bleedin'," he said.

"Don't do anything," Uzziah warned the younger brother.

Earl's younger brother watched his brother drop to the floor, he turned and went to the area between the cars. As they looked, there was a man alongside the tracks on a horse and holding two other horses.

"Why didn't ya throw the Bowie?" Immanuel asked him.

They all watched as the younger man jumped from the full-speed train. He tumbled over and over, but got up and ran back and jumped on one of the horses.

Uzziah pulled his Hawken from its leather case and ran to the area between the cars.

The two riders were riding obliquely away from the train. Uzziah primed the Hawken, then lay down on the platform between the cars. Immanuel came right behind and lay on the platform of the other car.

"Ain't never shot from a movin' train," Uzziah said.

"There's only one thing to remember," Immanuel said as he sighted in, "add the speed of the train and its movements to the shot."

"Oh," Uzziah said, "Is that all?"

In the passenger car, Gloria and Cassandra were leaning out the window, watching the whole business. Passengers were lined up along the windows on that side.

———

"What happened to Earl?" asked an older man who was old enough to be Earl and his younger brother's pa.

"He done got hisself kilt," the kid answered just as the older man's head exploded and his body sluffed off his horse.

"Pa!" the boy yelled as he turned and looked back at the dead body without a head. Just then, a 50-caliber lead bullet went through the boy's side, destroying his heart and lungs, then coming out the other side of him. He looked back at the train that was puffing smoke, and the last thing he heard was the sound of the braking train wheels, and the sound of two Hawkens.

———

The people on the train were cheering as they held on to their seats. The train was coming to a halt, slowly.

"Did you see that!" one man exclaimed.

"They must be sharpshooters with the Army," another remarked.

"I think that might be Jim Bridger, the famous mountain man," another said confidently.

The train had finally come to a halt. The woman who was sitting beside the man whom Earl shot was not related to him, though she did say he was a gentleman. Now, he was a dead gentleman.

The conductor opened the stock car for Immanuel and Uzziah. They rode out to where the three horses were wandering around eating mesquite.

"Did ya hear that one fool, said he thought ya was none other than Jim Bridger!" Uzziah said as they rode leisurely out to the horses.

"I did not hear that," Immanuel said.

"Yer hearing is shot, ya know that, don't ya?"

"What?"

"I said one of the gentlemen in the car we was riding in, said he thought ya was Jim Bridger."

"He did, did he?" Immanuel commenced to wondering.

"Stupid, huh?"

"No, I think it's brilliant. I will be Jim Bridger, and you will be Christopher Houston Carson."

"Who?"

"Kit Carson, ya dummy," Immanuel said as he rode along beside the old man's horse and, reaching down, picked up the reins.

"No one will believe that!" Uzziah said, securing the other horse, then he added, "Let's go get that other horse. This could turn out profitable-like."

"They'll believe it, if ya say it with enough conviction."

"I seen Carson's picture, he's a short, thin man," Uzziah said, not convinced of the plan.

"Just tell 'em ya gained weight since yer fame," Immanuel said, then remarked on the horses. "These fellas knew horse flesh that's fer sure!" Immanuel said as he got the third and final horse from the cadre of dead bandits.

The horses that were following Immanuel were a buttermilk dun and a black. Uzziah trailed a palomino behind him.

"We ain't really gonna lie to those nice folks, are we?" Uzziah asked.

"Why not, the railroad company'll probably give our monies back and all the men will want to buy us a drink!" Immanuel said as they rode within earshot.

"Oh no," Uzziah said under his breath.

All the passengers had exited the four passenger cars and were standing there giving the two men who had saved the day an ovation.

Immanuel, in his inimitable style, took his hat off and swept it toward the ground in a grand gesture. They loved it. More applause.

"I believe yer the one and only, Jim Bridger," the man from their car remarked.

"Then, sir," Immanuel said as he gave the horse he retrieved to the stockman, "you would be correct."

More applause, and some ladies screamed in joy, including the two soiled doves, who had pretty much figured out what was going on.

"And who is the man with you?" someone asked.

"Why that is none other than Christopher Houston Carson," Immanuel said, but the folks didn't know his whole name. "Otherwise known as Kit Carson, the infamous Army scout."

"But I thought Carson was thinner?" another man cut in.

"He was, alas, 'til fame bought him his corpulency!" Immanuel said, and everyone laughed uproariously.

The conductor had to get into the act. "The Railroad company would like to award Mr. Jim Bridger, and his sidekick, Kit Carson, the fine horses they were able to acquire from the bad hombres kilt so successfully on the plains," he said, and that statement too was greeted by thunderous applause.

"Such a magnanimous gesture, sir, how can we ever thank you?" Immanuel said as he got off his horse and handed the reins to the stockman.

"Join us for a free meal in the dining car, and your trip ticket price will also be refunded!" The conductor was really getting into it, thought Immanuel, and would probably be required to take that out of his own pocket.

7

They spent the next few days eating, drinking, and fornicating in the caboose, the brakeman insisted. And as the hills of the Appalachian Mountains began to be climbed, Immanuel turned to Uzziah, who had just put his pants back on. Gloria and Cassandra were both pooped, and were sleeping on the bunks in the caboose.

"Ya sorry ya brought me along?"

"What do ya think?" Uzziah said, pulling up his suspenders.

"Well, we have had a grand time of it, huh, partner?"

"Yeah, well, at that last water stop, did ya see the conductor hook up the wire, and send a message ahead?" Uzziah asked, wondering what would be waiting for them when they got to the station in the Shenandoah Valley.

"Nah, I missed that. Why ya lookin' so worried, every time, we hit easy street, ya get worried, that is not a noble sentiment."

"My guess is, when we get to the station, there will be a photographer there from one of the newspapers."

"So?"

"So, they will want to take our pictures for the papers."

"Let 'em!" Immanuel said, rolling a smoke from the makings which Gloria had in her reticule.

"Let 'em?"

"Yeah, let 'em," Immanuel said, putting his trousers back on.

"You realize they will probably know we ain't Jim Bridger and Kit Carson, right?"

Immanuel stood puffing on the smoke with his suspenders hanging down to the floor.

"Hadn't thought of that," he said sheepishly.

"Uh-huh, and what do you think will happen to us then?"

"I don't know, who cares?"

"I care!" Uzziah nearly yelled.

"Shush, you'll wake up the quim. Besides, if they take our picture and we manage to get away from the station without any trouble, even if they know we're not who we say we are, what harm will it do?"

"You've forgotten a certain lady who arrested me on the paddle wheeler?"

"Kate Warne!"

"Uh-huh, and when she sees our pictures in the paper, she'll recognize ya fer sure. Since ya shaved before ya saved me," Uzziah said.

"Then, we'll just have to exit the train early," Immanuel said.

"And how do we do that?"

"Simple, just follow my lead," Immanuel said, shrugging into the Spies 38s and their shoulder holsters.

They walked back to the stockcar.

"Hey, ya famous people come to give me some grief?" the stockman joked.

"No," Immanuel said, "We've come to reward ya fer takin' such good care of the stock," and he handed the man a good wad of money.

"No, siree, this is my job," the man said, trying to hand the money back.

"Keep the money. How long before we're at the station?"

"Well, we done slowed down fer the mountain climbs, and are startin' down into the valley," the stockman said as he opened the stock door and hung onto the holding ring.

"Nice view from here," Uzziah said as Immanuel went back and started saddling their two horses, and tying each of the ones they had been rewarded after the foiled robbery, jaw to tail, jaw to tail. Uzziah looked at the stockman and Immanuel grabbed him from behind, and put a chokehold on him.

"Easy, easy," Immanuel said as the man kicked and squirmed, but to no avail. "You're gonna go to sleep and have a nice rest," Immanuel said as the man passed out. He pulled him over and laid him in the hay.

Uzziah brought Immanuel's horses up, the one he was going to ride and the other two, tied to his D-ring.

"Now, when we jump, ifn they don't follow, we'll be in a world of hurt," Uzziah warned, then added, "We could just leave 'em here."

"No, these are fine horses and we're takin' every one of 'em. Now, come on."

"You go first, I'll stay back and urge yer two forward, I gotta a feelin' this palomino has had her nose up Shadow's butt since she got on board, she'll faller when we jump."

"Have it yer way, my friend," Immanuel said as he brought his horse up to the door. The wind was blowing in and the horse he was riding was snorting, but the train had slowed way down for the train yards.

Immanuel jumped, and the buttermilk dun was right behind him, but the black hesitated, and when he jumped, he landed oddly, and was limping around all over the place.

Uzziah was right about the palomino, she was on Shadow's arse, and they nearly jumped together.

Uzziah rode over to where Immanuel was down checking the black's leg.

"Broke?" Uzziah asked.

"'Fraid so," Immanuel said, and taking one of the 38s from his shoulder holster, he placed it right between the black's eyes and fired. She went down like a rock. "Now, let's get outta here!" Immanuel said and rode hard for the hills.

Uzziah sat his horse, looking at the fine dead animal.

"Sorry, gal, real sorry," he said, and he tipped his hat to her and put spurs to Shadow.

———

Heading for the hills is one thing, and not being at the railroad station is another, but something like what those two mountain men did on that train was not soon forgotten.

There was a great deal of disappointment when the newspapers had sent photographers and all, and a reporter to have the two tell their tale, and they weren't on the train.

The stockman told his story like this: "Well, they wanted off, 'cause you know they wanted to avoid the public eye. I imagine Kit Carson and Jim Bridger to be just like that, don't ya?" He didn't mention anything about being given a nap by Jim Bridger, it sounded better for everybody the way he told it.

They found the dead horse not far back up the line, and their horses' tracks which led to the hills, but why bother those two famous men? The newspapers took pictures of the dead horse, and got a sketch artist down from the paper to sketch pictures of the two famous men, and the story was entitled:

ROBBERS FOILED OF FORTUNE
By
Jim Bridger and Kit Carson

They sold a lot of papers, and it just so happened that Bridger was in Virginia at the time, visiting with his family. In these later years, he was known as Old Gabe, and he happened upon that story in the Alexandria Gazette. The storekeeper saw Jim pick up the Gazette and spoke up.

"Jim, when was you on a train comin' in from St. Louis?"

"Let me see and I'll tell ya," Bridger said as he scanned the paper. "Damn those boys, whoever they were had it goin' their way that's fer sure!" Bridger exclaimed, slapping his knee.

The storekeeper couldn't keep his mouth shut about hearing Bridger say that, and the next day, a reporter from the Gazette showed up at the Bridger family home in Richmond.

The door was answered by a negro in a butler uniform. "How can I helps you, sirrah?"

"Is Jim Bridger at home?"

"Yes, sirrah, he isn. Why don't ya come in and sit a spell whiles I gets him," the butler said, and the reporter sat in the parlor 'til Bridger came in.

"How can I help ya?" Bridger asked, his napkin still tucked into his shirt.

"Oh, I am sorry if I'm interrupting a meal—"

"Just spit it out, son."

"It's about this article in the newspaper, I was hoping you could fill in the missing gaps," the reporter from the Gazette said, holding the folded newspaper open to the article about the train robbers being killed.

"Come on in. Have some lunch and I'll tell y'all 'bout it," Bridger said.

The newspaperman felt he was going to get the scoop straight from Bridger's mouth, and he was. They settled down to scrambled eggs, country ham, country gravy, fried apples, and homemade bread.

"So, Mr. Bridger—"

"Call me Jim."

"Jim, how did ya get the drop on the train robbers?"

"Well, son, ifn y'all take a good look at the drawing of me, y'all see that ain't me!"

"Well, people disremember things, Jim."

"That's true, but that ain't me. And the other one, the fat Kit Carson, Kit ain'ts ever weighed as much as that man!"

"Then, who can these men be, and why didn't they want the notoriety?"

"Nobody wants to be famous, and it ain't something good in any case. The fat man in the drawing has a strong resemblance to a family I know in the valley."

"He does?"

"Sure does."

"And what family would they be?"

Bridger had a mouthful and was thinking whether he should tell the man about the O'Bannons. They were good Irish people, came over about the same time as his family. Did he want this vulture to pounce upon them or didn't he? He swallowed and looked at the reporter.

"I can't rightly remember their family name to tell truth, and it's probably just a bad drawing. I do know that ain't Christopher Carson, though, that's a fact."

"Well," said the reporter, taking a sip of the chicory flavored coffee, "that's too bad the railroad is trying to find these men, there's a substantial reward for foilin' that robbery."

"That so," Bridger said, knowing that farming families could always use seed money. "What ya callin' substantial?"

"I heard it was two thousand dollars," the reporter said, and was lying through his teeth.

"Hell, it was me on that train, I'll take the money," Bridger said, laughing.

"It was you, sir?"

"No, fool, it wasn't. That fat boy is a ringer for their oldest kid. He's gotten older, but I'd lay my hand on a Bible and say that was Uzziah O'Bannon."

The reporter got up without finishing his meal.

"Is there something wrong with the food, sir?" Bridger's mother, Chloe, asked.

"No ma'am, it's veritably delicious, but ifn I'm to catch the train back to Alexandria, I must hurry, my apologies, everything was wonderful," he said as he was heading for the front door.

"You take these," Chloe said as she made him two biscuit and country ham sandwiches, and wrapped them in a cloth napkin.

"I can't take your linens," the reporter objected.

"You can and you will," Chloe said.

"Thank you, so, Mrs. Bridger."

"Ifn I'm gonna be in the public papers, my Christian name is Chloe."

"Chloe Bridger, got it, and thanks," he said as the screen door slammed behind him.

"My, my, those city folks sure are in a hurry, ain't they, Jimmy?"

————

It was a hundred miles from Bridger's home in Richmond to Alexandria, Virginia, and the reporter missed the last train. He had to wait 'til the evening train. All this was unknown to Uzziah O'Bannon and Immanuel James Jones, but not for long.

————

Uzziah led the way. Well, he was going home for the first time in quite a few years. He sincerely hoped that his ma was still among the living, and he had always had a special feeling about his mama. He was her first-born and she had told him many times that she could tell when he was in danger and such. He wasn't quite sure that he believed her, not that he wanted to doubt his mama, but women will say things sometimes, they will.

As they rode the road which would end up going by his pappy's farm, Uzziah was getting excited and Immanuel just couldn't shut up.

"How many sisters ya got?"

"There was ten of us afore Ma quit havin' babies. Let me see there was Jake, the boy behind me, then Sally, she has hair the color of cornsilk, Raymond, he must be part black Irish 'cause his hair is like a raven's wing, then Samson, who is strong as an ox and actually quite short, but he don't have that feeling ya gets from some short men—"

"For God's sake, all I asked was how many sisters ya got, I don't want no by-the-book history of yer family!" Immanuel spat out.

Uzziah just looked at him, and the happy smile that had occupied his face disappeared, and he sat sullen in the saddle, looking straight ahead. They rode on for a bit.

"Don't ya think we oughta hurry, ain't yer ma sick?"

"We're nearly there, and rushin' never got anybody anywhere," Uzziah said.

"I bet yer ma says that."

Uzziah turned toward Immanuel and gave him the look. Immanuel had seen that look plenty of times, and he knew what it meant.

"Sorry."

"Where was I, oh yeah, Jake, pretty Sally, Raymond, Short Samson, but don't call him that 'til ya known him some, Zachariah, Hanna, Obadiah, Sarah, Faith, and John. I was the eldest and that's about it," Uzziah said, and he could see Immanuel counting on his fingers. "Save ya the trouble, there's four girls and six of us boys."

"Yeah, yeah, that's the count I got," Immanuel said, smiling.

"Now, I know how ya are," Uzziah said.

"What's that supposed to mean?"

"It means exactly what it means."

"Which is?!?"

"When ya gets into yer cups, ya become a hound dog when it comes to women."

"I resemble that remark," Immanuel joked.

"I know ya do, just let me warn ya—"

"What ya gonna do ifn one of yer sisters likes me, huh!?"

"Well, some'll be married, Sally was real strong on this one ole boy, and some won't, but it ain't me ya hafta worry 'bout."

"Yer pa, huh?"

"No."

"One of yer brothers then?"

"Not a one of them."

"Yer ma's sick."

"No."

"Then who?"

"Hannah."

"A girl?"

"She ain't no ordinary girl. Once, when Sally first started to date her beau, Frank, well, Hanna saw him kiss Sally, and she fired a gun at him as he was riding away from the farm."

"She what?"

"And she was only eight years old. I can't imagine how she'll be now, but family is scared of her, so watch yer step, brother."

"Duly noted," Immanuel said, wondering how Hanna looked, and if she were to like him, what would she do then?

"There it is!" Uzziah said and kicked up Shadow.

The two men were loping down the dirt road and up ahead on the left, with the Appalachian Mountains as backdrop, sat the O'Bannon farm. It was a good three hundred yards from the road, and when they headed down the winding dirt road that led to it, Immanuel was impressed. To the north sat the home, two buildings joined by a third, which was one-story and probably just a hall. The barn was painted red and had a tin roof, which was in the gambrel style. There was a silo between the farmhouse and another structure where probably Uzziah's pa stored the farm equipment. All in all, it was quite an operation, it seemed to Immanuel.

———

A man in his teens walked out of the barn area and saw the two riders coming fast.

"Pa, two men ridin' in fast!" Obadiah yelled.

From the barn ran Sean O'Bannon, fifty-three years old and in amazing shape. His long reddish beard touched his belt, and the short-sleeved long underwear he wore showed his massive arms and bulging muscles. Behind him ran John, twelve years old and holding a pitchfork, then Raymond, who had left a mule in the field with a plow, and Hank from the house with a rifle.

———

"We'd better slow down, the family looks worried about us," Uzziah said, and both men brought their horses to a dogtrot.

"Who are ya, and what do ya want?" Hank, twenty-four years old, yelled down the road at the two men and at the same time, racked a round into the chamber of the Winchester.

"Wait, Hank, I think we know the younger one," Sean said as he ran down the road toward the two men.

"Who does Pa know who would be ridin' in like that?" John asked Hank.

"It can't be," Hank said.

"It can't be what?" John asked.

"It sure can be!" Faith said. She was ten years old when Uzziah left, and now at fifteen, she looked every bit a woman as Hanna, her nineteen-year-old sister.

Hanna came from the house, drying her hands on a dish towel.

"What's goin' on?" Hanna asked.

"Somebody Pa knows," John said, his hand up to his eyes, shielding them from the glare of the sun.

Meanwhile, down the road, Uzziah had dismounted and ran toward his pa. The two men ran into each other, and Uzziah picked his pa, Sean, up and whirled around with him.

"Son, son, it can't be ya!" his pa yelled as he was sat back down on the ground.

By then, Hank, John, and Hanna were all running down the dirt road.

"It's Uzziah!" Hanna yelled.

"Yes, it is!" John joined in. "He looks smaller than

when he left," John said, running with the pitchfork in his hand.

Fairly soon, John, Hank, Hanna, and Raymond, with his shoulder-length raven hair, joined their father in a group hug of the big mountain man, Uzziah, who had been gone for the last five years.

"I got Ma's letter, how is she?" Uzziah asked.

"She's still bedridden, but Doc says she'll come around. She will be so glad to see ya," Sean said as he thumped Uzziah on the chest. All there were smiling and hugging, then Uzziah looked up at Immanuel, who sat his horse, and he, too, was smiling at the happy family reunion.

"Oh, Pa, John, Hank, Hanna, Raymond, I want ya to meet my best friend in the world, and my partner, Immanuel James Jones," Uzziah said.

Immanuel dismounted, ground-tied his horse, and walked the short distance to the group of five people he'd just been introduced to. He went directly to Hanna, who was nineteen years old, with fiery red hair which was gathered behind her head but flowing all around her at nearly waist length, and he picked up her hand, and raised it to his lips and kissed it gently. It was like she was the only one there.

"Madam, I am thrilled to meet you, and hope that we will become the closest of friends," Immanuel said, then turned to the others as Hanna got back her hand and looked at it. "And, of course, the same to you, gentlemen, but I'm assumin' ya wouldn't want me kissin' yer hands."

Sean, John, Hank, and Raymond all laughed and in line shook Immanuel's hand.

"Any friend, or partner, for that matter, of Uzziah

O'Bannon's is a friend to all of us," Sean said. "Welcome to the family."

Uzziah noticed the fiery Hanna still holding her hand as if it were a sacred relic. Immanuel had worked his magic once again.

"Now, come, boy, yer ma hasn't a clue, although she may have heard us a shoutin'," Sean said, as Uzziah grabbed the reins of Shadow and his trailing horse.

"Where's Obadiah and Short Samson?"

"Well, Short Samson had a growth spurt after ya left, and he's taller than all of us, Obadiah, well, he's only seventeen and he raised up the alarm when ya came ridin' in fast, but the boy, well, I don't know, to tell the truth. There he stands over by the barn where he first saw ya, and Short Samson, we still call 'im that, he's on the roof of the barn tarring up some leaks."

Short Samson, standing tall on the roof, must have recognized Uzziah because he was screaming, "Welcome home, big brother, welcome home!"

As they walked toward the barn and stables where they'd put up their horses, Uzziah turned to John, who was following him like a pup.

"I brought ya somethin' if ya want it," Uzziah said to John as he gathered him to his side.

"You were bigger when ya left," John said, and Immanuel cracked up.

"My God, boy, if he was bigger then, I'm glad he shrunk!"

"What ya think of this horse?" Uzziah asked John.

"The black?"

"No, that's my horse, Shadow, and no man can ride him but me."

"Really?"

"Ya better believe him, boy, there's many a man that's tried and failed," Immanuel said.

"No, I'm talking this palomino I have trailing after Shadow, she's yers ifn ya want her?"

"I'd rather have the buttermilk dun that Mr. Immanuel is draggin'."

"Sorry, pal, that dun belongs to Hanna," Immanuel said, and Hanna ran into Immanuel's arms screaming, then taking the lead rope off Immanuel's horse, jumped on the dun and rode bareback and without a bit down the road away from the house.

"How come everybody's gettin' somethin' but me!" Faith demanded.

"We won't see Hanna fer a bit," Uzziah's pa said.

"I guess she can ride," Immanuel said, scratching his head at the hat line.

"Ain't anybody hearin' what Imma sayin'!?" Faith veritably yelled.

"Here, this has been my favorite piece of Injun jewelry forever, but lookin' in those beautiful green eyes, I can see it belongs 'round yer neck," Immanuel said as he took the Injun necklace he nearly always wore and put it around Faith's neck. She screamed and kissed him on the cheek.

"I'll be glad to have the palomino, brother, I've already got a name fer her," John said.

"And what name would that be, boyo?" his father asked.

"Holy Ghost," John said.

"Don't be tellin' yer ma ya named a horse that, she'll have yer hide fer breakfast," his father said.

Back in Alexandria, Virginia, the reporter who had visited the real Jim Bridger had finally made it to the Gazette. He and his boss had been talking since he arrived back on the train.

"You look a mess, Baldwin, where have you been?" his boss asked.

"Mr. Turney, ya won't believe this, but I went to see the real Jim Bridger."

"Get more of that story about the train robbers, did you?"

"No, Mr. Turney, Bridger was nowhere near that train. It was a man from the Shenandoah River Valley named O'Bannon, he was the one who said he was Kit Carson."

"And who was impersonating Mr. Bridger?"

"I don't know, but I want yer permission to go into the valley and look for this O'Bannon."

"You've already spent a lot more time on this story than it needs."

"Sir, if I may, there's a lot more to this story than meets the eye. I think those two men didn't ride into the train station because they wanted to avoid the publicity."

"Well, it galls me that more people aren't interested in their privacy, to tell you the truth."

"But, Mr. Turney, I think there's more to it. Please, just another day or two and I can have a much bigger story than that, I'm sure," Baldwin said.

"Okay, but it better be good," Turney said. "Now, get out of my office. I've got work to do."

———

The house was quiet and dark. People in Virginia knew that pulling back all the curtains and letting in all that light in the middle of the day did nothing but make a house hot. The blinds had been drawn to keep out the sun and the heat, and the house was as cool as a root cellar.

"Yer ma's in her room, I think ya should go up by yerself," Sean said.

As Uzziah climbed the staircase to the second story, he was taken back many, many years. He was just a boy when his pa, Sean, had added the second story to the house, and his ma was so proud that she could have a room up where the breeze blew. He built her a really big bed chamber with closets on both ends. The closet on the right, as you walked in, went all the way through to something that hardly anybody had at the time, a bathroom. There was a bath in there, but it was also like an outhouse. The shite just dropped two stories to the hole below. Every year, Sean would take the doors off the bottom of it, pull out the shite, and put lime down there. It was a convenience, and since she had been sick, with God knows what, it had been a real blessing.

The main thing was across from the foot of the big bed. There was a porch which had two rocking chairs on it, and Sean and his wife, Rahab, yes, like the whore in the Bible who had not given away the spies when they snuck into the city, and it was considered to her as righteousness, sat there in the evenings, and even during her convalescence, she managed to get out there and rock. She would watch the trees down by the stream blow in the wind, and just seeing those leaves turn in the wind, one side green, the other silver, was a blessing to her.

There wasn't much light in the room, since the curtains were drawn, but the wind was blowing the curtains out into the room, and only the screen door to the porch was closed. Uzziah walked in, and it seemed as though she was sleeping. She was propped up by several pillows and there had been a book in her hand, but it had closed and was lying lower than her open hand.

"Mama," Uzziah said real low.

She stirred in the bed as if she were having a dream.

Uzziah sat on the bed and his mama stirred a bit and made a moaning noise.

He took her hand in his, and her eyes opened.

"I died, didn't I?" she said as she looked at her oldest boy. "But that must mean ya died out in the mountains. Oh, son, I'm so sorry. How did it happen?"

"Mama, I ain't dead, and neither are you."

She looked around. "Well, thank heavens fer that, thought heaven might be just a bit higher livin' than the farm." She sat up, and they hugged.

"Oh, son, ya got my letter, didn't ya?"

"I did, Mama."

"Let me look at you. Well," she said, fingering the fancy vest and coat material, "I guess mountain men dress better than we imagined."

Uzziah chuckled. "You could always make me laugh, Mama Rahab," he said.

"Ain't nobody calls me that 'cept you."

"Pa says yer gettin' better."

"That's what Doc Collins says, but I still don't have much energy. Those poor kids are havin' to do everything on their own."

"Well, the important thing is that you rest."

She flung the covers back and started to stand. She was dressed in her housecoat, which was the only thing Uzziah could remember her in when she wasn't properly dressed. It hung just above her ankles, and there were darts on the side which allowed for her bosoms, but it was pretty much a simple house dress.

"Mama, no, what are ya doin'?"

"I am gettin' up and fixin' you yer favorite meal of fresh pork loin, sweet taters, and string beans from the garden. Plus, the whole family will like this, I'm making my biscuits!"

There was no stopping her, so Uzziah held her arm as they made their way down the hall, then down the steep stairs. Uzziah went first in case she fell. Nothing was going to get past that hulk of a man.

When she appeared in the kitchen, where everyone was sitting around the huge kitchen table and being regaled by Immanuel's stories, everyone stopped and looked at her as if she had just come from the dead.

"Mama's back," Faith said, then ran to her. "Lookie at the necklace that man there gave me, it's real Indian jewelry!" she said as she showed it to her mother.

"That sure is nice, honey. Now, y'all stop lookin' at me like that. I am not dead, and I will not be dying today, just get outta my kitchen, so's I can fix a proper, well..." seeing Immanuel, she stopped talking, and her hands went to the top of her housecoat. She pulled Uzziah aside.

"You didn't tell me we had a houseguest, son!"

"He's my partner, let me introduce you."

"Hanna, stop gawking at that man, and help me get back upstairs, I am not properly dressed," Mama commanded, then she turned to Uzziah. "You tell that gorgeous older man that I will return in all my splendor," she said as she looked over her shoulder at him one last time. "My, my," she said as Hanna came to her side and helped her through the parlor.

———

Wasting no time, and riding their way in a buggy was Baldwin Munford. He hadn't had a story like this ever, and sitting beside him was the best photographer at the Gazette. It was an eighty-mile ride, and they had brought along a tent to stay one night on the way.

"Now, Charlie, this man may not want to be photographed. As a matter of fact, he may resent that we have even come to visit him," Baldwin said.

Charlie wasn't old, but he was a drunk. The only reason the Gazette put up with him was that his photographs were stupendous. He was able to catch people when they didn't know he was taking the cover off the lens, and some of his pictures were the first to show people in natural ways. He hated photos where everyone was smiling, or no one was. He liked to relax his subjects and sometimes, if they were still enough, he'd take the lens off and hope and pray that they wouldn't move for the required amount of time. Telling them not to move just made them into corpses. Such was Charlie Brandon's idea of a good photograph. He didn't mind shooting pictures of dead men—they rarely moved—but thought it below his station, even if it paid the same.

"Whatever ya say," Charlie said as he sipped his bottle of rye.

"And don't get drunk on me, ya hear?"

"I hear, boyo, but really, what is drunk, I ask you?"

Baldwin just looked at Charlie and wished there was someone else who could have done this.

"I don't know, either," Charlie said, then added, "I gots me an idea about this picture. If ya can get the man I'm gonna photograph interested in something which he isn't supposed to see, like a naked lady, perhaps, or a man about to blow his brains out, then he'll stand as still as a corpse and show us his true self."

"You do have some of the strangest ideas." Just then, they were passing a caravan of gypsies, they had pulled to the side of the road to water their horses, and one of the gypsy girls was dancing around like no one was watching.

"Stop, stop!" Charlie ordered.

Baldwin pulled the buggy to a stop.

"What is it now?"

"That gypsy girl back there, we need her to come with us. If we could get her to dance like that when she thinks no one is watching, then we'll get the photograph ya want, and he won't even know it's happened."

8

Uzziah's mother had come down about a half hour later, and she was dressed as if she was going to church. Sean O'Bannon looked at her like she was crazy. She had Samson kill a pig and get her enough pork loin to feed them all. He had to kill two of them, but that was fine because they would smoke the rest of the hams.

"I can't believe it," Sean said to Uzziah, "she's all dressed up and cooking to beat the band."

"It's Immanuel," Uzziah admitted.

"What's ya mean, son?"

"He has this—I don't know—animal thing about him which all women love."

"So, yer telllin' me yer ma got up out of her sick bed and got all fancied up to flirt with yer partner?"

Uzziah just shrugged.

"Say, where's Sarah?"

"She's at school. Can't get me boys interested in learnin' but she just loves it," he said and looked at his pocket watch. "She should be home any moment. Says she wants to be a teacher when she grows up."

"Ain't she grown by now?" Uzziah asked.

"She just turned sixteen, *U*."

"Oh," was all Uzziah said.

It was just then that Sarah came in and saw Uzziah. She ran and jumped into his arms.

"My big brother, how are you?" she asked as he put her down.

"I'm fine, and you?"

"Well," she said, "well, who's the hunk on the front porch entertaining everyone, and Mother!" she yelled, "what are you doing cooking in that dress, for that matter what are you doing cooking at all, here let me do that," Sarah said as she took the spoon from her ma.

"Where's Immanuel?" Uzziah's mother asked him.

"In on the front porch tellin' lies."

"Good, I love a good lie," she said as she exited the kitchen.

Uzziah sauntered over to the stove where Sarah had taken over like she had begun the whole process.

"How'd ya get her to let ya help?"

"You don't ask that woman, you just jump right in," she said, smiling.

"Where's Sally?"

"She got married to that Cummins boy, Frank, and they moved up to Harper's Ferry."

"Oh, is she happy?"

"Got a little baby girl, name Bonnie, not that any of us have that name, yeah, I think she is happy. Faith went over there last Christmas and enjoyed herself, of course, that Cummins boy made over her, which made

Sally mad, and Faith got sent home. This family, I swear."

"Well, I'll be," Uzziah said, starting to put his finger in the gravy.

Sarah slapped it hard with the wooden spoon. "No, you don't!"

"That hurt."

"It was supposed to, idiot!" she said and leaned into him. "It's so good to have you back."

"What's with Obadiah?"

"He's just a queer duck," she said and said no more.

"Ya mean as in queer, queer?"

"No, I mean as in the ugly duckling kind of queer. He thinks he should have been born into one of the plantation families with the Grecian columns and the slaves."

"Ya got to be kiddin'?"

"No, but he'll come around."

"How do ya know?" Uzziah asked.

"See any fields of cotton in the Shenandoah Valley, see any big plantation houses?"

"I gotcha," Uzziah said as Immanuel came in.

"Yer ma wants me to help her set the big dining room table, where's the silver?"

"This is Immanuel, my partner, and speaking of thinking he's on the plantation, the flatware is in that drawer," Uzziah pointed out. "Ya want me to help?"

"We can get it, Rahab and I," Immanuel said as he grabbed two handfuls and headed for the formal dining room.

"Mother's having him call her by her Christian name?" Sarah whispered to Uzziah.

"Yeah, well, ya hafta know the man, and his powers over the feminine persuasion."

"That might be fun," she joked as she finished making the gravy and looked in the oven at the biscuits.

"Don't even say that," Uzziah said.

"Only kidding, brother, you've forgotten my sense of humor, haven't you?"

"Maybe, but speaking of senses of humor, I got an idea," Uzziah said and started to leave the kitchen.

"Don't go far, this will be on the table in five minutes," Sarah said.

"Only going to get the old man," Uzziah said, and he walked out the kitchen door and headed for the barn.

Obadiah was in there with their pa, and when he saw Uzziah, he scooted out the side door and headed for the house.

"What's with him?" Uzziah asked his pa.

"He's been like this since the beginnin'. Thinks he was born a Prince and we stole his body from the Kingdom," Sean joked.

"Say, Pa, ya still makin' yer own shine?"

"Ya haven't said a word to yer ma, have ya?"

"No, no, it's just I think it would be great for Immanuel to taste real homemade shine," Uzziah said.

"Which should I bring? X, double X, or the dynamite?"

"Bring a bottle of X for us, and we'll let Immanuel drink the dynamite."

"Oh, son, ya haven't lost yer terrible sense of doing a body wrong, have ya?"

"Nope, don't think so," Uzziah said, toting both jugs, one in each hand.

"Say, I was noticing yer horse," Uzziah's pa said.

"What 'bout him?"

"Well, he's a fine horse, but where's Molly?"

"Pa, she got kilt by some bad hombres that me and Immanuel dealt with."

"Hope ya dealt deadly with 'em."

"We did."

"Yer a good boy," Sean said, slapping his son on the back.

Supper started out with Uzziah saying grace and everybody saying how he should have been a minister, and Immanuel recounting how many times the boy had put people under and read from the Good Book, and how once he'd said the 23rd Psalm from memory.

All this time, Uzziah was pouring Immanuel a good, healthy drink from the dynamite jug and handing it to him, and he'd down it and keep on talking, then Uzziah would hand him another and so on.

Sean was smiling so big. Things like this tickled the people from that part of Virginia like they were born to it.

"What ya grinnin' at, Pa?" his wife Rahab wanted to know.

"Just great to have the boy home, that's all."

"Ain't it, Pa?" Faith said, fingering her new native necklace.

"So's, I gots to ask ya, Rahab," began Immanuel, and his face was getting red, "why would yer ma name you after someone in the Bible who had a reputation?"

All got quiet, it was a subject that was usually not broached, and here Immanuel had ask.

"Well, she admired women with color in their lives, and especially women who helped men in trouble. Tell truth, I think that's how she got my pa anyways. So I did take a thump or two in school over it as I was growin' up, but gave as good as I got. Most folks just call me Ra and leave it at that, which I guess I am at times," Uzziah's mother said, and everyone laughed.

"We just can't believe how ya got up off yer sickbed and did all ya did," Sarah said, and all the children nodded in agreement.

"Reminds me of when Jesus came to Peter's house, and Peter's ma was sick and she got up and fixed them all something to eat," Uzziah said.

"I do hope you are not comparing yerself to our Lord and Master," Uzziah's mama interjected.

"No, ma'am, a course not, but ya did git up and fix this tremendous meal," Uzziah said.

"Proof's in the puddin'," she said.

"Ya made puddin'?" John asked, and everyone laughed.

"What's so funny?" John wanted to know, and they laughed again.

The bowls, family style, were passed around, and the talk got quiet as the plates were filled, and the eating began. Uzziah kept refilling Immanuel's cup and he kept right on drinking. He was slouched a bit in his seat.

"How long ya gonna stay?" Hanna asked.

"Sort of depends, don't it, Immanuel?"

"Huh?" Immanuel looked up. "Did somebody say somethin' to me?"

"Leave the poor man alone, he looks peaked," Faith said.

Sean and Uzziah chuckled and Mama O'Bannon caught on. She got up from her place at the table and walked over beside Uzziah and his pa.

"Yer not supposed to bring that brew in this house, outside in the barn is one thing, but really, Pa, how could you?"

"It was my idea, Ma, fergot yer ways 'bout it," Uzziah lied.

"You poor fella," Ma said as she patted Immanuel on the shoulder. "How much of this have they fed ya?"

Immanuel looked at her like she was from another planet, then she shook his shoulder, "Young fella?!" she shouted at him, and he looked up and smiled, then oozed right out of his seat onto the floor.

"Immanuel!" screamed Faith as she got down on the floor and started fanning his face with a napkin.

"Well, I never, a body starts havin' some fun after being sick and you two go and spoil everythin'!" she said, looking at Uzziah and Sean. "Raymond, Obadiah, ya grab him gentle-like and place him on the couch in the parlor, understand?"

"But Mama, I'm eatin'," Obadiah objected.

"He speaks!" Zechariah said, and the whole table erupted in good-natured laughter.

Mama went over to Obadiah, grabbed him by the ear, twisted it, and got him out of his seat. "Now, do what I tell ya, help Raymond with our distinguished guest."

"Extinguished would be more like it," Short Samson said, and the table erupted again in laughter, even Mama forgot her manners and laughed out loud.

"Poor, poor man," Faith said, still fanning his flushed face.

Sean got up and went to Mama. "That's the first time I heard that there laugh since ya got sick, I do believe yer on the mend, old woman." He kissed her right on the lips, which got catcalls and hollering from the kids.

"What happened!? What I miss!?" Immanuel asked, sitting up from his position on the floor.

"He's all better," Faith said, grabbing him around the shoulders. "It was my fannin' that done it."

Then Immanuel's eyes rolled back in his head and he collapsed, this time taking Faith with him.

"We haven't had this much fun for such a long time, won't you stay, Uzziah?" Sarah asked.

"Mayhaps, little missy, mayhaps," Uzziah said, helping Faith up off the floor.

———

Unbeknownst to the family O'Bannon, Baldwin Munford, and the photographer from the Gazette, Charlie, had pulled into the fields opposite the O'Bannon farm, and the gypsies were right behind them. The whole plan had been explained by Baldwin to the old gypsy man, and his granddaughter. They were to start playing music, the old man on the squeeze box, and the girl was to dance around like she had when Baldwin first saw them.

Charlie was setting up his camera in a grove of apple trees, hidden from view. Charles had made his own telescopic lens from a design by Peter Barlow. It was heavy and cumbersome, and had to have its own leg to keep the camera from falling over. He set everything up, and pointed it at the place on the farm where the men would have the best view of the dancing gypsy girl. Her name was Esmeralda and she was a mere slip of a girl, only sixteen years old. But the outfit she danced in was skimpy and the veils she twirled with were enhancing. Baldwin knew that they would get a picture, then an interview with Uzziah before tomorrow was through.

They slept well, and Baldwin watched the house from which so much laughter erupted from time to time that he almost regretted disturbing them, almost.

———

Uzziah was up with the sun, and Immanuel still was asleep or unconscious on the parlor couch. When Uzziah came down to the kitchen, as usual, like in the old days, his mother was up and cooking grits, bacon, sausage, biscuits, fried apples, country ham, red-eye gravy, fried potatoes, and she even had a coffee cake in the oven.

"Mama, shouldn't you be resting?"

"Oh, son, I'll sleep when I'm dead," she said as she kissed him on the cheek. "It's just so good to have ya home, I barely slept last night, thinkin' of all the food I'm gonna prepare fer ya and poor Immanuel."

"Mama, I am sorry about last night, me and Pa—"

"Now, Uzziah, haven't ya been taught to take the blame when the blame is for the taking? Yer pa said it was yern idea and he just went along with it."

"He said that, did he? Where is the old man anyways?"

"In the dern barn, acourse, where'd ya think he'd be?"

The smells of the breakfast brought all the children down at once, almost. As usual, Obadiah was last down the stairs, and he sort of kept to himself.

"Ma, Obadiah?" was all Uzziah said.

"He's an odd duck, that's all. He'll come round, don't ya worry about Obadiah. Ya gots to 'member he was named after a man whose name means servant of Yahweh, and I think he is just that. 'Member he was the man who hid the prophets in two caves, so that if one cave was discovered, the others might live. His righteousness was considered one step higher than that of Abraham, our father," she said.

"Does he know all this?"

"Well, yes, when he was but a squirt, I read him the book of Obadiah," Rahab said and smiled, then added, "Since it was only twenty-one verses long, he's memorized it by the time he was six years old."

"I remember ya readin' to him, but I didn't know," Uzziah said, looking at Obadiah, who was sitting at the table with the rest.

"Sit, son, sit," Rahab said to Uzziah, and the only place left to sit was beside Obadiah.

"Brother, how are ya?" Uzziah said to Obadiah, who looked askance at his older brother but said nothing.

"Cat got yer tongue?" Uzziah asked him.

Obadiah simply pointed his head toward their father, who was ready to bless the food. All joined hands, except Obadiah, who held his hands to the side of his head, palms toward the sky.

They all dug in, and Immanuel was happy to have something to eat, since he'd been robbed of supper by the drink he'd taken.

"What's goin' on inside that head of yourn?" Uzziah asked Obadiah.

"As you have done, it will be done to you. Your

deeds will return upon your own head," Obadiah said, quoting the book which he had memorized.

Uzziah was about to say something, but there was a racket outside, coming from the next farm, or at least their fields. Sean went to the window to see.

"Lord have mercy," he said, and that brought half the table to the window.

"What she doin' out there?" John asked.

"They call that exotic dancin' in St. Louis," Immanuel said, "I'm gonna take a better look," he said, and walking by the table, grabbed a couple biscuits, opened them up, and put slices of country ham in them.

"Is the whole world gone mad?" Rahab asked.

"Come see, Ma, it looks like she ain't got any bones," John exclaimed.

That was enough for their mother, she was up and at the window, when she saw what the girl was doing, she grabbed John by the ear and pulled him away, "No son of mine will be watchin' that pagan dance, since when do we have gypsies in the valley?" she asked anybody who might listen.

"I'm gonna go tell 'em to stop," Sean said.

"Yeah, I'll help ya, Pa," Raymond said.

Obadiah looked out the window once, then fell on his knees and started praying.

"Maybe she could teach me how that's done?" Hanna said and went with the older men outside.

"Hanna, ya come back here this instant!" her ma yelled, but it was on deaf ears.

By the time they all got out there, the closest they could get was the neighbor's fence, which was about thirty-five feet from where the girl was whirling and gyrating around in the grass. The old gypsy was playing a squeeze box and the rhythm of the song fit perfectly with the undulations of the young girl.

"Hot damn!" Immanuel exclaimed, and was joined by his partner, Uzziah. They both stood frozen, almost in tableau as they stared at the dancing girl.

Sean was yelling, but the gypsy girl and the old man paid him no attention.

"Stop it! Stop that heathen dancin', right now!" Sean said, and the girl smiled beautifully at him and he shut up.

Hank was enthralled, and all the O'Bannon men looked as if they had been hypnotized.

Off in the grove of trees, Charlie, a bit lit even at this time in the morning, was replacing plate after plate, hoping that the two they were after in the picture would be in focus in one of the shots.

"Have ya got 'em?" Baldwin asked.

"Shhh!" was all Charlie said as he pulled an exposed plate and put in another.

Then a shot was fired over the head of the old man and the girl, when everyone turned around, it was Rahab. She held her husband's old gun and was reloading it.

"Mother, what are ya doin'?" Sean asked his wife.

"Somethin' that it seems ya are unable to do!" she said, and pointing the rifle at the gypsies again she fired it and it came perilously close to the girl's foot who was dancing. The gypsy girl screamed, and ran to the caravan, the old man got up on the driver's box and whipped the horse into running away with them.

"Well, I'm guessin' the dancin' is over," Hanna said. "And just when I think I was gettin' her steps down," she said, returning to the house.

The rest of breakfast was eaten in silence as Mother O'Bannon glared at her men and boys. Obadiah was still praying aloud in the corner by the window.

"Will ya shut yer yap, ya damn fool!" his mother shouted at the boy. He looked at her and his expression was one of hurt as he ran from the house, the screen door slamming. "And how many times do I hafta remind ya, stop slammin' that door!"

Immanuel looked at Uzziah and they were chuckling inside.

"Where's the lad goin', if I may ask?" Immanuel said.

"To his cave," Uzziah's mother answered and said no more.

9

Kate Warne was sitting at an outdoor café in St. Louis, drinking hot tea and smoking a dark little cigarette. She was waiting for her breakfast that she had already ordered. Sitting across from her was her partner, much to her dismay, Tom, whose last name she could never remember, thank God. He was drinking American coffee and thought hot tea was for the British, but he wasn't about to tell Miss Warne that. He'd been practicing his marksmanship in the hills around St. Louis and thought that he had become better at it. Actually, he was always good at hitting targets, but when it came to a man who might shoot back, Tom was a terrible shot. He figured quite correctly that his days as a Pinkerton Agent were few, and he was right. He'd only gotten the job because his sister knew the sister of Allan Pinkerton, and she persuaded her brother as a favor to hire the man.

As she thumbed through the edition of the Missouri and Illinois Baptist, a rag of a paper which reran almost all articles from other papers, and were days old, when she jumped up so fast that she knocked over her tea, and Tom was up with his pistol drawn.

"Tom, put yer wee weapon away," she said. "We've got to get to Virginia!"

As she ran off, he picked up the newspaper she'd been reading and looked at the headline of the article:

REAL HEROES OF THE RAIL

Below the headline, there was a picture, a bit blurry, but still recognizable, of Uzziah O'Bannon and James Jones Immanuel, who were standing with some other folks, all looking at something which was not in the picture.

When he caught up with Kate Warne, she started in. "They been posing as Jim Bridger and Kit Carson for God's sake, who in their right minds would think they two clowns were those great men!"

When they got to the train station, she got two tickets for the Shenandoah Valley, and she was in luck, the next train was in two hours.

———

Uzziah's visit with his sick mother was going well, but the two mountain men had forgotten just how much they enjoyed each other's company and just about no one else's. This made Uzziah feel a bit guilty, but for the past five years, he had maintained a lifestyle which was—to say the least—not much like farming.

A week into their visit, they were getting ready for the trip back to the Rockies. His pa, Sean, had jerked a lot of meat, and Immanuel was busy making pemmican.

Sean had become interested in it, and Immanuel was showing him how it was done.

Obadiah had finally come down from his caves and was again helping the family, but hardly talking to anyone.

The real interest—certainly among the boys—was Shadow. Short Samson had a bet with Zachariah that he could ride Shadow, and Raymond swore he could without a doubt. Hank knew enough about horse flesh to know that that stallion was a brooding storm ready to happen.

"What about you, Hank, yer good at ridin'?" Faith asked her older brother.

"Thanks, but no thanks," Hank said.

"Chicken," Zachariah said, and Raymond started flapping his arms with his hands up under his armpits and scratching the ground with his feet while he clucked.

"I'd rather be called chicken than get a broke arm," Hank said, but it didn't look much like he cared for the teasing.

"Leave old brother alone," Faith said adamantly.

"Old, yeah, that why, he's old," Raymond said, still parading around like a chicken and clucking between words.

Uzziah walked into the paddock area and everybody shut up. He put a halter on Shadow and then threw the blanket up on him, then the saddle, cinched it right up, led him around a bit, then cinched it tighter, then he stepped up on the horse and looked at his siblings.

"This horse is a stallion and he will buck you off if

you ain't me, and from where I'm sitting there ain't nobody but me, who's me!" he said and laughed.

Immanuel walked over and spoke low to all the other brothers. "Don't even think about it, please."

"That's it, I'm riding the horse," Raymond said as he climbed the fence, his raven hair bouncing around as he jumped down from the top rail. "Come on off, brother, Shadow has now met the man who will be the second man to ride him." Raymond stood there and looked up at Uzziah.

"It's yer funeral, as the saying goes," Uzziah said as he stepped off Shadow and handed the reins to Raymond. "But wait just a minute, I wanna get outta the way."

Uzziah walked to the fence and sat up on the top rail, his boot heels hooked on the bottom rung.

"Does anybody wanna place a bet?" Immanuel asked.

There was a flurry of action as money was taken, an IOU was taken, promises of payment were made, and Immanuel stood there holding the bets.

"Looks like even money to me," Immanuel said.

Raymond put his left foot in the stirrup, pulled himself up, and leaned across the saddle. Shadow looked around at Raymond's arse, and then straight ahead again.

"Looks like he don't mind," Raymond said as he threw his right leg over and sat aside the big black horse.

"Ya see, nothin' to it," Raymond said as he kicked up Shadow and started riding him around the paddock area.

Cheers went up along with some groans from those

who had lost. Uzziah stayed right there on the fence, watching.

"Yer gettin' overconfident, Ray, overconfident," Uzziah said, slipping back to the other side of the fence out of harm's way.

"What ya doin' that fer, he's as gentle as a kitten," Ray got those words out, then Shadow started running in circles in the paddock. Ray hollered like he was having the time of his life, then Shadow came to an abrupt stop, with Raymond resting on the big horse's head. Shadow flipped his head back and put Ray back in the saddle.

"See that, we're best friends—" that's all Raymond got out when Shadow skyrocketed up about fifteen feet in the air, and coming down on straight legs, snapped Ray's head to his chest, and a groan went from Raymond as Shadow started sun fishing and wiggling all over the place. The minute Raymond thought he had a seat, it would be taken from him, and the horse would go into a different mode of jumping. Raymond's head was snapping back and forth off his chest, then thrown back as far as a neck can be thrown before it snaps. Finally, Raymond just let go and was flung over the paddock fence and into a pile of horse dung. He lay there as if dead, then everyone rushed over. He was alive, but hurting. The boys carried him into the house and laid him down in the backroom off the kitchen.

"What's happened to that boy?" Uzziah's mother asked.

"He tried to ride Shadow," Hank said.

"Why didn't you stop him?!?" she asked Uzziah, who shrugged.

Raymond awakened and he moaned as if he were dying.

"Don't let anybody else get on that crazy horse," he muttered, and they all laughed.

———

A few days passed, and Raymond was better. He wouldn't be his old self again for a time. Both his eyes were blackened, he couldn't raise either arm above his shoulder, he walked with a limp, and he had double vision for a day.

"Partner, we gotta be goin' and that's all there is to it. Yer ma is fine, and I'd sure hate it if something else happened to one of yer kin because of us," Immanuel said.

Uzziah had been sitting on the front porch with his mama, who was sleeping in the hammock. He looked out on the green rolling farm and all the kids, his brothers and sisters, who were making a go of it with his pa and ma. The road had a lot of dust coming off it, and he nudged Immanuel, who was sitting in the other rocking chair. Immanuel looked where Uzziah was looking and the dust was hot and heavy on the road leading to the O'Bannon farm road.

"What ya suppose that is?" Uzziah asked, kissing his mama on the forehead, and she didn't wake up.

"Whatever it is, it's too many fer us to handle. Let's get our horses," Immanuel said.

The two men went through the house and headed out the kitchen door to the barn. His pa was in there, and so was Obadiah. And Obadiah was kneeling in the corner of the barn, praying.

Immanuel took the spyglass from his saddlebags, while Uzziah explained what was happening to his pa, both of them started saddling three horses, Uzziah's, Immanuel's, and one for Obadiah.

"It's that lady from the paddle wheeler, that Pinkerton lady, and I use the term loosely," Immanuel said, still looking through the glass. "And she's bringing the US Army with her! There must be fifty of 'em!"

Obadiah was in there praying and Uzziah went over to him. "Obbie, ya gotta help us, take us to yer cave, okay?" Uzziah said, sounding frantic.

Obadiah looked up and said nothing.

Immanuel grabbed him and stood him up.

"Ya gotta take us now to those caves of yourn, understand, holy man!" Immanuel said.

"They's comin' fer us, and they will probably shoot up the family in the process," Uzziah said.

"Okay, let's go," Obadiah said as he ran and mounted up on his horse.

The three men went out of the barn about the same time Kate Warne, Tom, and the US Army were starting down the O'Bannon dirt road toward the farm.

Sean O'Bannon was not unfamiliar with the law. He had seen what the law had done to some of his German neighbors when they had taken in one of their kin who was running from them. He was determined to keep them here talking as long as he could to give Obadiah time to get to his cave. He, thankfully, didn't know where those caves were, but he had an idea. They were on the other side of the mountain that the O'Bannon farm nestled up against, then over a couple more, and that's all he knew.

He was wiping his hands from greasing a wheel

when the fifty-some horses came in, raising a cloud of dust that he knew his wife would be livid about.

"Afternoon," he said in a slow drawl. "How can I help ya?"

Kate Warne looked around like she was ready to kill somebody or something. "Where's yer son, Uzziah!?"

"My son, Uzziah, ya say?"

"Yes!" she screamed and rode toward Sean, who did not move or even put his hands out to keep the horse away. "If ya don't tell us, we'll tear the place apart, understand?!?"

There was a blast from a Greener and it tore over Kate Warne's head like a thousand yellow jackets. She ducked, drew her gun, and was trying to get her horse settled down, as were the Army soldiers, when she turned the way the shot came from. There stood Rahab O'Bannon, the Greener smoking in her hands.

"What is the meaning of this? Firing on officers of the law, and the US Army!?!" Warne demanded.

"My name is Rahab O'Bannon," Uzziah's mother started in, "perhaps, instead of comin' in here and makin' a week's worth of dustin' fer me and my girls, then almost runnin' my husband down with yer horse, ya might have the decency to calmly tell us what this is all about!"

Kate put the pistol away when she saw the children of Rahab O'Bannon standing behind her. Each of them was armed all the way down to the twelve-year-old John, who held a flintlock, which probably wasn't loaded.

Kate rode her horse over to where Mrs. O'Bannon stood. "Ma'am, do you have a son named Uzziah O'Bannon?"

"You know we do, or ya wouldn't be here."

"Is Uzziah here?"

"No, he left a couple of days ago. Why do you ask?"

"Ma'am—"

"My name is Rahab, you may call me by that name."

Sean was loving how his wife of nearly twenty-eight years was handling this officer of the law. He was so proud, he wanted to go right over there and kiss her, but he decided to wait to see what Rahab had in mind.

"Your son, Uzziah, and his accomplice, Immanuel James Jones, are wanted for the killing of a Pinkerton Agent by the name of Robert Spells, and they are also wanted for disabling a paddle wheeler on the Missouri River after Mr. Jones helped Uzziah escape from my apprehension of him."

"Sounds like the boy was busy."

"Don't make light of these charges. He will swing for the first charge and probably go to jail, if he lives for the second."

"How did Mr. Spells, ya say, how did he die?"

"What difference could that possibly make?"

"Just curious, that's all."

"He froze to death in the Rocky Mountains."

"And my son got him to do that, how?"

"It's not important, the original charge against both Jones and O'Bannon is the murder of an undersheriff, Randall Hicken, deputy to the high sheriff in Saint Louis, Missouri."

Rahab O'Bannon looked at the sky. It was getting late, the sun was retreating behind the western mountains that encircled the Shenandoah Valley.

"Won't ya come in and have some supper, all of ya,

and we can discuss these charges and where my son might have gone to?"

Kate Warne knew when she had been outmaneuvered. This farmwife had kept her in conversation for the last ten minutes, and even if her boy and the one accompanying him had just left, they would be where? Perhaps, it would be best if they made camp right there tonight and proceeded in the morning.

"We will gladly accept your invitation. Lieutenant, have your men bivouac out there in that field. Would that be acceptable, sir?" she asked, turning to Sean O'Bannon.

"Yes, ma'am, and please tell the men they may graze their horses at their leisure," he said, smiling his best Irish smile.

10

Obadiah wasn't happy about showing his secret cave to his brother, Uzziah, much less a total stranger to him. He didn't care that Uzziah said the man had been his partner for the past five years. That could mean that he had been his partner in crime, couldn't it? Why had the US Army come looking for them? What had they done to enrage an entire nation against them? Obadiah was getting madder and madder by the second. They had only crossed the first ridge, and there were two more to go. He came to his senses and whoaed his horse.

"I don't know ya," he said, pointing directly at Immanuel.

"Well, of course ya don't. Ya've just met me, how could you say ya know me?"

"And I ain't sure who ya are anymore, either," Obadiah said, pointing now at his older brother.

"That's my fault, ye were only twelve when I left, so far down the rungs that we hardly had any interactions. I'm truly sorry," Uzziah said, taking a look at their backtrail just in case.

"What have ya done to bring the authorities down on us all?" Obadiah asked.

"We kilt a man, who kilt a lovely young girl that we both loved," Immanuel said, "And I can't say now, or then that I'd take it back, the man deserved to die, and we dun him in, fer sure!"

"Thank ya fer being honest, it's more than my brother was able to do."

Uzziah looked at Immanuel, who shrugged. It was his universal way of saying, *Oh well, old son, we done it now.*

"Will ya take us to yer cave, or should we strike out now on our own?" Uzziah asked humbly.

"No, yer still my brother, even though yer a murderer, ya know when Ma hears this it's gonna break her heart, right?"

"Maybe, son, and maybe not," Immanuel began. "A ma's love goes deeper than any man can feel, y'all grant me that?" Immanuel looked at Obadiah and shook his head, he did agree. "Your ma lets ya run to the hills when ya feel like it, I'll bet ya did it when she was sick, too?" Again, Obadiah shook his head in agreement with that statement. "Then, who's to tell how yer ma will react about whatever they tell her? I think Rahab has a mind of her own. Now, take us to the cave, please, so we can rest, make plans, and move on out of yer lives, perhaps forever."

Obadiah didn't say anything, he just kicked up his horse and kept riding toward his cave. Uzziah raised his eyebrows to Immanuel, who only smiled.

Back at the O'Bannon farmhouse, things seemed to be returning to normal, well, under the circumstances, as normal could be. Kate Warne was enjoying some tea with Rahab O'Bannon, and everyone was hovering, hoping to find out exactly what this was all about.

Sean O'Bannon had gone back into the barn and was pretending to grease more axles, but he kept a wary eye on the US Cavalry. They hadn't taken their horses into the field which he had granted they could stay. They had dismounted, but each cavalryman was standing beside his horse, and they were talking with one another.

There was one man who had not dismounted. He was an Indian. He was big and powerful, and Sean had heard him be called Abooksigun. He looked way more intelligent than the rank and file of the Army, and was riding around looking at the ground. When he rode up behind the bar, he yipped and rode back to the house.

Kate Warne was explaining why the US Cavalry and the US Army were interested in Rahab's son and the man called Immanuel James Jones, who rode with him. She had just started her story when an Indian ran into the room.

"Three horses, shod, into the hills behind the barn, fresh tracks," was all Abooksigun said, and he disappeared back outside.

"I am sorry, but we have to leave. Thank you so for your hospitality, Rahab, it's been rather enlightening getting to meet you," Kate said as she finished her cup of tea and walked swiftly from the house.

"Mount up, we're moving out!" Kate yelled, and her orders were followed.

Abooksigun led the way up into the hills behind the barn, and nearly fifty horses followed him.

———

The three men, Immanuel and the two brothers, rode smartly up the next ridge of mountains, and were about to crest the ridge when Immanuel reined in his horse, turned it, and pulled his spyglass from the saddlebags behind him.

Uzziah and Obadiah stopped and looked back at him.

"What's wrong?" Obadiah asked.

"He's just being careful, checking the back trail," Uzziah assured his brother.

"Damn!" was all Immanuel said as he turned his horse and they took off down into the next valley. As they rode, he came up alongside Obadiah.

"How much further to yer cave?"

"It's in the next set of ridges?"

"Is it easily spotted?"

"No, I purposely chose a cave which I had barely found the first time."

"Are there other caves?" Immanuel asked.

"Those hills ahead are honeycombed with them," Obadiah said.

"Good, now we must hurry, they're not but a few miles behind us," Immanuel said, and he kicked up his horse.

Uzziah rode up alongside as they looped down into the next valley. "How bad is it?"

"They got an Injun tracker, that's how bad it is."

"Good thing we left Samson back at the hostlers in St. Louis or he'd bring them right to us," Uzziah said.

"That Injun looks like he knows what he's doing. They might not need Samson to find us, now come on," Immanuel said as they reached the floor of the valley.

The last few trees were whizzing by them, and the ground ahead looked fertile and good for riding. Uzziah just hoped the groundhogs weren't in this area, and if they were, one of them was shortly to find out. They galloped three abreast, their hats flying back as the fronts of them bent in the wind of the gallop.

Uzziah looked over at Obadiah and he was smiling like it was Christmas. Who knew anybody? The boy had said some things that made Uzziah think that he wanted to turn them in, and now, he was full tilt in the run away from the law. Blood was thicker than water, and for that, Uzziah was elated.

They ran upon a small lake, and instead of riding around, Immanuel went on into the lake.

"This will slow us down," Obadiah warned.

"Yeah, but they won't know which way we've went 'til they find our tracks again."

The three horses got to the lake and they rode right in. When they got to deep water, Immanuel spoke. "Don't rein them at all, let their heads be free. They like swimming, but aren't very fast, about as fast as a man can walk. Let their heads move the way they move, take your feet from the stirrups, and lay out behind by grabbing the saddle horn."

All three did just that and it was amazing to see them swimming alongside each other.

"Won't they catch up with us if they see us?" Obadiah was worried.

"If they see us, and there are so many ifs it's not worth talking, just enjoy the coolness," Uzziah said.

Immanuel kept sneaking a look behind them, and then he said, "I'm going to change directions and go off to the left. Don't worry, your horses will follow mine."

He was right, and Uzziah wondered how he had changed the direction of the horses' swim, he would ask later. It didn't take them long before they were on the shore. All the horses shook like dogs when they got out and then Immanuel kicked his horses into a gallop.

"You take the lead now," Immanuel shouted back to Obadiah, as he brought his horse to a halt and brought out the spyglass. He glanced behind them.

———

Abooksigun ran his horse to the edge of the lake. He looked out on the lake.

"Do you see them?" Kate asked him.

"No, but they rode into the lake and swam with their horses."

"Lieutenant, take half your men and go around the right side of the lake, we will take the left. Abooksigun, come with us," she said as she took off around the left side of the lake.

———

A storm came in, it came in suddenly and with much force. The wind was blowing hard, and the low clouds scudded close to the ground.

Suddenly, Immanuel shouted, "Go back to the lake, now!" Then, he made a circle and rode quickly back to the lake.

"What are we doing now?" Obadiah yelled at Uzziah as they headed after Immanuel.

"Who knows, just trust the man's instinct, brother, trust it!"

When they got back to the lake, Immanuel rode right in and rode back in the direction they had swum in the first time. The other two joined him, and they all three held on, laid out, and let the big animals with the huge lungs float and kick their way to where they had entered the water. It was less than twenty minutes and they were back at the same spot where they entered the lake.

"Now, we ride into the tracks of the fifty horses that followed us," Immanuel said, and he did just that.

"But my cave is in the opposite direction," Obadiah objected.

"Exactly," Uzziah said, smiling. What a brilliant partner he had.

They rode all the way to the first valley, then turned south and rode hard and away at an angle toward the second valley. Within an hour, they had made the ridge of the second valley, which led into the third, and they could see the lake off to the north of them about three miles.

Immanuel took out his spyglass and began laughing. "Beautiful, beautiful," he said as he handed the glass to Uzziah.

What Uzziah saw was indeed beautiful. The entire troop was gathered at the western end of the lake and the Injun was down on the ground trying to decipher their tracks.

———

Abooksigun sat back on his heels and contemplated what he was seeing. Kate Warne rode up and shouted at him. "Well, which way did they go, Injun!?"

He looked up at her and said nothing.

Finally, she rode up beside him and swatted him with her quirt. "You dumb savage, which way did they go!!"

He grabbed the quirt and pulled it from her hand, it almost pulled her from the horse.

"Well!?!" Kate screamed at him.

He looked up at her. "I understand yer anger. These men that you chase, they are not ordinary men." He paused and looked at Tom, who was riding beside Kate Warne. "But you, sir, already knew this. They have vanished into the tracks of two hundred horse hooves, and I do not know where to begin."

"Well, ain't that just swell!" Warne said, and then hung her head. Tom sat taller in the saddle, if they would outsmart this Injun tracker, then he didn't feel so bad about being played for a fool back at the paddle wheeler, no sir, he sure didn't.

———

Obadiah led them to his secret cave. He felt okay about showing them because they were going back to the famous Rocky Mountains, and would surely not have time to reveal to anyone in the Shenandoah where his cave was. He built up a nice fire way back in the cave, and he told the other two men—one his brother, Uzziah —that the smoke hole in the cave vented into a groove of dogwood trees, and when it finally reached the top, it was so dissipated that it couldn't be seen. After all, they did call these mountains the Smokies.

About ten o'clock that night, a weary troop of US Cavalry rode down from the mountain behind Sean O'Bannon's farm.

The family heard them ride in, and Sean put his hand out, telling the rest of the family to stay. Rahab followed him out regardless.

"Do you still need the field to bivouac in?" Sean asked the lieutenant.

"Yes, sir, we surely do," he said, and he led his men into the field and closed the wooden gate behind them.

Rahab O'Bannon was searching the troops for her captive sons and Immanuel, but they were nowhere in sight. She did see Kate Warne, who looked like she'd been to hell and back.

"Can I offer ya a featherbed for the night, Miss Warne?" she said in a most pleasant voice.

"Yes, ma'am," Warne said and actually managed a little smile.

"I'll take yer horse and put him in the barn," Sean O'Bannon said, and taking the reins, he helped her off her horse, and she followed the mother into the house. Shortly afterward, as Sean came from the barn, Mother O'Bannon came out of the house.

"Is she tucked away?" Sean asked.

"Yes, have ya seen the Injun that was with them?"

"He's camped a little ways from the troops, but in the same field," Sean said.

"Don't suppose he's in a teepee?" she said and smiled. He chuckled as he kissed her before she walked off.

In the field, Abooksigun had seen everything. Kate went into the house to have her comforts, the mother came back out, and now, she was coming his way, as all mothers will do.

"Am I bothering you?" Rahab asked before she sat down by the small fire he'd built.

"Please," was all he said.

She sat across from him and studied his face. "I do a little sketching from time to time, do you have the time in the morning to sit fer me?"

He smiled. "I am on Great Spirit's time, and would be honored," he said.

"Good, good." Then she looked at Abooksigun and just looked.

"You have a squaw way about you."

"Thanks, I guess."

"Want to know what happened, right, Mother Squaw?"

"Yes, I do."

"Don't worry, your sons and the man they ride with are like ghosts."

"They're dead!" she exclaimed and clasped her hands over her mouth.

Abooksigun immediately came and sat beside Rahab. "No, Mother, they live and will continue to live as free as I once did."

"What do ya mean?" she said, taking her hands down from her mouth.

"They are white Indians. They will live as free as they want, don't worry, Mother Squaw. Your sons and the man they ride with are safe from any harm brought by that woman." When he said that, he looked disdainfully toward the house. "And these pups"—he made a gesture toward the cavalrymen settling in—"someday, this US Cavalry will ride with too much pride where they do not belong. It will be a great battle and a great defeat."

"How do you know?"

"I have eyes," was all he said.

———

That night, as they ate a supper that Uzziah fixed for them, Obadiah looked between the two men as the three of them ate around the campfire. There was a peace between the two men that Obadiah wanted badly, and he had no idea how they got it, or if they even deserved it. The manner in which they joked with each other, and even sometimes calling each other bad names, like mountain nigger, and even stupid, well, Obadiah had never seen anything like it. He wanted that peace.

"Ya got any whiskey in this hole in the ground?" Immanuel asked Obadiah.

"No," Obadiah said with a smile.

"What's ya grinnin' about mountain nigger?" Immanuel said.

"You called me that, thanks," Obadiah said and smiled again.

"Yer kin is off center, ain't they?" Immanuel asked Uzziah.

"A bit, but so are all the Irish."

"True that."

"I want to go with you." There, Obadiah had said what he had wanted to say for the past hour. He did want to go with them, anywhere, he didn't care. The way they had escaped the US Cavalry was so...so... amazing, so, literally wonderful.

Immanuel looked at Uzziah, who had his head down in his plate and was sopping the gravy from the rabbit stew onto a biscuit. Uzziah finally looked at his brother Obadiah and sighed.

"No, you don't," he said softly.

"Yes, yes," Obadiah said as he jumped up and started dancing around the room, "I've never wanted anything so much in my whole life, really!"

"Yer seventeen, son, a pup, wet behind the earholes," Immanuel said kindly, "but we do take it as a compliment to two murderers."

"I shouldn't have said that, and I am truly sorry," Obadiah said.

"Well, I don't know about you, Uzziah, but I am greatly and forever relieved," Immanuel said, chuckling.

"We're gonna go through the Shenandoah and say goodbye to Mama and we'll settle it then," Uzziah said.

"What!" both Immanuel and Obadiah said.

"We are not gonna go back the way we came, we are not!" Immanuel said with a great deal of resolution.

"It would be crazy, brother, they might be lying in wait fer us," Obadiah agreed.

"Crazy or not, a Virginian does not leave his mama

without sayin' a proper goodbye," Uzziah said, folding his arms across his chest.

"Oh no, when he does the arm foldin' yer in fer a fight, that's fer sure," Immanuel said, then added, "Ya sure ya ain't got whiskey?"

"There's whiskey, shine, and or whatever else ya might want just three ridges to the west," Uzziah said, arms still folded.

"That's true," Immanuel said.

"I will not go back and see Mama," Obadiah said, resenting that he would have to.

"Uh huh, ya know don't ya?" Uzziah said.

"What's he know?" Immanuel asked.

"Ifn he goes back and says to Mama what he said to us, she will box his ears," Uzziah said.

"I am nearly a growed man, she will not do that to me!" Obadiah said.

"You watch," Uzziah said.

"Oh, good, then we will go back through. I love family drama, especially this family's," Immanuel said.

"You changed sides," Obadiah said, looking at Immanuel with contempt.

"Yep, sure did, pup."

11

Kate Warne was saying her goodbyes to Rahab O'Bannon, and the US Cavalry were all mounted up and ready to go.

"The bed, last night, oh my, haven't been that comfortable since I was at the Westchester in New York City," Warne said, trying to impress these simple country folk.

"Well, I'll bet the Westchester charged you a lot more than I'm goin' to!" Rahab said and cackled like a hen when Kate Warne's eyes nearly bugged out. Then the two women had a laugh, and Kate mounted up with the help of the lieutenant. She wasn't riding side-saddle, which was the custom of the day, but nothing surprised women who had ridden by forking the saddle since they were little girls.

Rahab and Sean stood with their children and waved as the cavalry rode away.

"Oh, I just think that lieutenant was so handsome, didn't ya, Mother?" Sarah asked.

"I guess in a kinda cavalier sort of way," her ma said.

"Look, they's leavin' the Injun behind," Sean noted.

"Probably to spy to see ifn Uzziah returns," Hank said.

Rahab looked at Abooksigun and he at her, then he rode a ways off, and getting off his horse, settled himself under a tree.

"Ya see!" Raymond noted. "Hank's right."

"Want me to go throw him off the property?" Samson asked his pa.

"What do ya think, Mother?"

"Abooksigun is fine, I ain't worried 'bout him at all."

Sean looked at Rahab, and she turned and looked back at him.

"How ya know that Injun's name?"

"We talked last night."

"What?"

"You heard me, now I gotta fix something fer these hungry children to eat fer lunch," she said and walked back into the house.

"Pa?" Hank inquired.

"When yer married, y'all understand," Sean said and walked toward the barn.

"Yeah, Hank, when yer married," Hanna teased. "Y'all understand that we womens is the boss."

"Hogwash," Hank said, and he went back to get the mule to plow the rest of the lower fields.

"Ya really believe that, don't ya?" Faith asked.

"A'course, I do," Hanna said, then added, "Ain't seen a man I'd kowtow to."

"Ain't seen a man that'd let ya do such a thing," Raymond said and ran just as she picked up a rock and nailed him in the back with it at thirty yards.

"Damn! That hurt," Raymond complained.

"Meant it to, fool!" Hanna yelled back.

"You children stop this foolishness and get to yer chores!" It was Mama, she was at the kitchen door, and everybody scattered.

———

Meanwhile, on the road back to Strasburg, Tom rode up alongside Kate Warne, who was riding with the lieutenant.

"'Cuse me, ma'am," he said.

"Yes?" She turned, annoyed that she would have to listen to this incompetent.

"Ya really gonna leave an Injun to watch and see ifn they comes back?"

"Don't be silly, we've put our best sniper in the western hills, if they come back, one of them will surely die," she said and went back to talking with the lieutenant.

———

Back in the trees, mostly laurels, some dogwoods, serviceberry, redbud, locust, and sourwood trees—the Appalachians having the greatest variety of trees in almost the entire world—a single cavalryman tied his horse to a chestnut tree and climbed high into it. The higher he got, the better he was able to see the entire O'Bannon farm. This cavalryman was the recipient of a Whitworth rifle, one of the first used in the field. It was an experimental rifle and it had an iron scope which allowed the sniper a range of close to 1,500 yards, eight-tenths of a mile. It was muzzle loaded, and a good marksman could reload in about twenty seconds, which would equal three shots per minute.

He perched himself high up, but not high enough to be bothered by the occasional breeze that would come along assuredly.

Once there, he found a notch made by a branch coming out from a limb, and he rested the end of the almost three-foot rifle in the notch and rested the butt of it in his lap as he awaited what might happen down at the O'Bannon farm.

———

Down at the farm, Abooksigun knew they had sent a sharpshooter into the western mountain opposite the farm. The Indian's vision was excellent, even though he wasn't a young man. He watched closely to see the movement of a tree that moved without the aid of the wind. He saw such a thing and reckoned correctly that the sharpshooter would be in that vicinity, even though he couldn't see him.

One of the O'Bannon children had brought lunch to him, friend chicken and biscuits, which he had had once before, and thought it was the best of the White man's food. He enjoyed himself immensely and licked his fingers clean of the buttery chicken grease, even enjoying that.

He thought that sniping, as it was known in the white man's world, was a ghastly and unheroic sort of killing. To shoot someone when they least expected it, what kind of valor or courage was in that sort of killing? The Algonquin tribe from upper New York State, a tribe of which he was a member, would never do such a thing. In fact, screaming while attacking was their way of giving their enemies advance warning and preparing them to fight. Courage was won when equal opponents fought to the death. This other means of shooting from the next village seemed cowardly to Abooksigun, and he would have nothing to do with it.

The late afternoon heat, combined with a full stomach, had the effect on Abooksigun that it would have on any man, he fell asleep under the shade of the tree. There was a light breeze that cooled him and he was having a very nice dream about a squaw that he once desired but was taken by another brave. In the dream, she had come back to him and was telling him what a mistake she had made, and asked if he would allow her into his teepee. He was opening the teepee flap, she had gone in. What a lovely behind she possessed, and just as he was about to join her, he heard voices, white men's voices.

That's when he awakened, and looking up toward the house, there stood Uzziah, Obadiah, and Immanuel, talking with Uzziah's mother, Rahab. Their father, Sean, was walking from the barn, and when Abooksigun turned and looked toward the trees on the western slope, he knew what was about to happen.

He picked up his rifle and fired it into the air.

———

Everyone there at the kitchen door and standing near the grape arbor that led to the road ducked when they heard the rifle shot, and a bullet grazed Obadiah's shoulder between his head and the shoulder. He screamed out in pain.

Uzziah looked down to where the Injun had fired his weapon, just as the report of another weapon accosted them. The Injun was pointing to the western slope on the other side of the farm. "There he is, see the smoke!" Immanuel shouted. "Scatter, he'll have to reload."

Everyone went into the house except for Uzziah and Immanuel. They ran to the stone wall which separated the road from the yard and laid down behind it, plenty of cover. As they were gathering their Hawkens together, Abooksigun ran up and lay down, just a shot splattered against the stone wall.

Immanuel looked up and so did Uzziah and Abooksigun.

"The smoke, there!" Abooksigun shouted.

"I see it," Immanuel said, as he sighted in.

"Ya only got another ten seconds," Uzziah said.

"Shut up!" Immanuel said, then, letting out his breath, he fired the big gun. "Now, we wait."

They waited for ten minutes.

"Maybe he want target," Abooksigun said, and stood up.

"Get down, ya damn Injun!" Immanuel shouted.

Nothing happened.

"Well, ya was with them," Uzziah said, and he stood up and stuck out his hand, "I'm Uzziah," he said.

"Abooksigun," the Injun said.

"Glad to meet ya," Uzziah said, then turned to Immanuel. "He ain't shootin', partner."

"Well, they had to have heard both rifles, let's get outta here," Immanuel said.

Mama O'Bannon, her husband, Sean, and all the kids ran out and hugs went all around. Obadiah was bandaged and Mama was holding onto him. Then, the two men mounted up, and so did the Indian.

"I go with you," he said.

"They's gonna faller us," Immanuel said.

"Can't follow ghosts," Abooksigun said, and they rode off together.

Less than ten minutes later, the US Cavalry came riding down the road to the O'Bannon farm.

"What happened?" Kate Warne asked.

"Nothin'," Sean said, he was out there shoveling manure into a barrel.

———

They sent a cavalryman up to where the sniper was and they found him. His leg was caught in the branches of the chestnut tree, and there was a hole in his body and blood was dripping to the ground.

They sent advance troops down the road south and they returned no tracks that were fresh. They went east and west and nothing.

"Where could they have gone?" Kate Warne asked no one in particular.

And Rahab remembered Abooksigun's words, *"Can't follow ghosts,"* and she smiled.

12

They got a train somewhere around Lexington, Kentucky, that took them all the way to St. Louis. They had an argument with the conductor about the Injun riding with the rest of the passengers, so they rode with him in the stock car. Wasn't a bad ride, considering.

They got their horses out the minute they got to St. Louis, and Abooksigun got some looks, but he was with two of the strongest and biggest men in the city, and he was no lightweight himself.

"We gotta get more money, Uzziah?"

They looked at the Injun.

"No wampum here," he said and actually smiled. First time they had seen anybody smile about being broke. Who knew, maybe he had some, but wasn't sharing?

"Missionary teach me read, look sign," he said.

There, as plain as day, was a sign announcing a horse race that very afternoon, talk about the luck of the Irish. It was down by the railyard, from there to two miles out of town and back to the railyard. There would be a judge there to make sure the winner made the turn at the right place.

"What's ya think?"

"Shadow?"

"A'course."

"With me on top?"

"Won't let anybody else ride him."

"What the hell, what's the entry fee?"

Turned out to be every cent they had, not including the Injun who was probably holding out on them. The race was at sunset, and the riders would be riding back with the sun in their eyes.

They had lunch at The Growling Cat, and Abooksigun got himself a white poke, his first.

Immanuel and Uzziah sat and had a beer while the Injun was poking. When he came out, he had a sour expression on his face.

"What's a matter, couldn't get it up?" Immanuel asked.

"No, he stand high and mighty," Abooksigun said.

"Then what?" Uzziah asked.

"Like when they smell less like fish and more like bear grease."

The boys wouldn't touch that one, but said he should try again just to see if he had more money, or wampum as he called it.

"Would rather catch fish," he said.

So, they went down by the river and borrowed three cane poles off these kids, promising them that they would give them whatever fish they caught.

They were hooting and hollering so that the time got past them, and when they looked, it was fifteen minutes before the race, and the money they'd put down would not be refunded if they didn't show. They had told Charlie Waters about the race, and when they rode to the train yard, there he was.

"That's the horse I'm bettin' on," Waters explained to one of the bookies, he laid down a pile and explained to the boys that if he won, he'd stake them back to the Rockies and if they lost they'd have to work for him whether they were wanted by the law or not.

"I no part of this," Abooksigun said, letting Charlie know he wouldn't be working in the fish market.

The horses that were to race were paraded with their riders up and down the easement of the railroad. Betting was heavy. There was a thoroughbred or two there with skinny jockeys and saddles that looked like postage stamps. The mustachioed men who owned those horses stood by their jockeys and laughed at Uzziah's girth.

"Don't ya pay 'em no mind, old son, ya hear," Immanuel whispered in Uzziah's ear.

"But them riders weigh less than my brother Johnnie, and he's only twelve years old!"

"Shadow is fast, there ain't any two ways 'bout it, have some gosh dern faith, boy!"

"But he's been runnin' mostly from Injuns and gunfire," Uzziah explained.

"Good things to run from," Abooksigun said, and it was the first time they knew he was standing there.

"No offense?" Uzziah said.

"No taken," said the Injun.

It was race time, there were about fourteen horses in the race, those two thoroughbreds and lots of quarter cow horses, a clown from the circus in town was riding a zebra, and the betting was furious around that striped equine and its jovial rider, and there was even a woman in the race, dressed to the nines in a black long dress, pearls around her neck and a derby on her head. Then, there was the mountain man who looked like a grubby gambler who had gone to seed and whose belly was the biggest talk of the race.

"I hear the fancy gal ridin' sideways is high in the instep," Immanuel said.

"Riders, mount your ponies!" a man yelled through a tube which was small on one end and big on the other.

"He yell with teepee in mouth," Abooksigun said, and that got Uzziah laughing when the gun went off. Shadow was standing there and everybody was laughing. Finally, Shadow took off, but he was at least fifteen lengths behind the last horse.

"I go help," Abooksigun said, and rode off on his horse.

Immanuel looked after him and wondered what the hell that could mean.

Halfway to the turnabout, Uzziah had managed to get on the tail of the losing horse. The field was filled fairly evenly with cowboys and jerks, with the clown on the zebra right behind the two thoroughbreds.

At the turnabout, the zebra took the turn too sharp and the clown got his clown suit caught in some wire or other that projected from the turnabout box. He flew off like a party favor, with his red rubber-gloved hands outstretched to catch his fall and his overlarge clown shoes taking an early exit and hitting the lady riding side-saddle in the face. She lost her concentration and fell, too, and nearly got herself trampled to boot. The zebra just kept on running. The two high-dollar horses were up front coming down at the three-quarter mark, and the big shots were twirling their mustaches, wondering who would win.

Then Immanuel saw Abooksigun sitting his horse at about that point, three-quarter mark, and he wondered what the Injun had in mind.

Uzziah had passed all the cow ponies and disgruntled cowboys like they were standing still, but he still hadn't reached for that extra step he was capable of. Then, Abooksigun kicked up his unshod pony and ran outside the raceway, firing his pistol and whooping it up.

"Yip, yip, yip, yip, Aieee!" he screamed like a banshee on the hunt, and Immanuel saw Shadow take a quick glance at Abooksigun, and that's when he reached down and gave it the blast.

The jockeys on the high-dollar ponies looked at Uzziah like he was from a bad dream they were having. The money men's mouths were open, and cigars already lit in victory were tumbling from gaping mouths into the dust.

Abooksigun's run couldn't have been more than fifteen yards and he pulled up and got lost.

To his dying day, Immanuel would never forget that mountain nigger's smile as he crossed the finish line a good three lengths ahead of the money horses. If he'd had dentures, they would have been in the dirt. Immanuel didn't know a person could have that big a smile.

There was a lot of cussing and tearing hair out, but no one seemed to have noticed the Injun acting like an Injun. They must have thought he was just a drunk redskin partying it up.

Charlie Waters was happy as a whoremonger, which of course he was, but the pile of bills in his hand reminded Immanuel of some sort of statue that celebrates wheat harvests. Abooksigun had put his wampum, which he swore he didn't have on Uzziah, and the three men rode away from the race a bit happier, but not as happy as when they were fishing.

They were about halfway through the train yards and Shadow was still heaving a bit in the chest when this fella stepped out between two railcars and held up his hand. The three riders came to a halt. He wasn't drunk, or if he was, he held it well, but he had a single Walker Colt tied to his left leg, and he was dressed all in black like an undertaker. His mustache was pencil thin, and it looked a bit like it had been drawn on his upper snarling lip.

"That there's my brother's horse," he said calmly.

"Beg pardon?" Uzziah said politely.

"Ya deaf?" the man in black asked.

"What ya say?" Uzziah was too happy to be serious.

"I said—" he caught himself, seeing Uzziah was making fun. "Get off my brother's horse," he said a bit louder this time.

"No, won't do that, 'cause if this is yer brother's horse, he was a no-good, side-winding, floor-flushing, double-dealing, woman-raping son of a bitch!" Uzziah just laid it out there, so to speak.

To their surprise, the man dressed all in black with the pencil mustache said, "So, ya knew my brother?"

"That I did," Uzziah said, his hand getting closer to his pistol.

"Did ya kill him?"

"No, but I didn't lose no sleep when I seen him hanged."

"You'd better get off that horse afore I kill all three of you sons of squaws!" he said, and he went for that low-slung gun, but before he could clear leather a tomahawk was sticking out of his forehead. Neither of the mountain men had seen it fly there, but there it was!

He stood there, his gun half from the holster, blood running down his nose, glided by his septum into his mouth.

"Fuckin' Injun," was all he said as he crumbled to his knees, like a cake taken out of the oven too soon, then over backward so he looked as if he was in the middle of doing some acrobatic maneuver. A spout of blood pontificated into the air, making a momentary pink cloud burst over his oddly positioned body. He was dead!

Immanuel and Uzziah turned and looked at Abooksigun.

"Squaw, Algonquin word for quim," he said, and riding up, he got off his pony, retrieved his tomahawk and danced around the body singing something in his native tongue, then quick as a flash, he had his big knife out and was pulling the dark hair off the head of the dead man.

"Aieeeee!" he screamed as he held it up over his head and looked to the heavens.

That's all it took, Shadow broke into a run.

"Whoa, whoa, whoa!" Uzziah yelled, but to no avail.

They caught up with Uzziah outside of town. Shadow had calmed down and Abooksigun was smiling.

"Good horse, know when run," he said, and Uzziah and Immanuel looked at each other and started laughing. Finally, their laughter was so real, the Algonquin joined in. They stopped several times, but one of them would start back up and all three were lost in the laughter. At long last, perhaps a couple miles, they had stopped laughing.

"First good laugh in years," Abooksigun said, and the two mountain men started back up again.

EPILOGUE

They thought he would stay with them, but when they saw the mountains looming on the near horizon, Abooksigun brought his horse to a halt. Neither of them noticed for a while, and when they turned, he was twenty feet behind them.

"Thought ya was comin' to meet Flying Feathers?" Immanuel said.

"No, must see land of vapors," he said.

"Yes, yes," Immanuel said, "the Land of the Burning Ground, you must see it, that's true."

"You go before?"

"Many, many moons ago."

"Worth trip?"

"Trip of a lifetime," Immanuel said, smiling.

"Good," he said as he turned his horse and started to ride off, then he turned on the horse. "You good men," he said, and turning back, he rode away.

EPILOGUE

SACRIFICIAL LAMB

These three things amaze me, no four are a wonder to me: The way of an eagle on the wind, the way of a snake on a flat rock, the way of a ship on the high seas, and the way of a man with a maiden.

— PROVERBS 30:18-19

1

They had watched Abooksigun ride off, and they both thought, much to his credit, he continued to look forward until they could see him no longer. It was probably an Injun trait or at least one which the Algonquins respected. Your life is not in the past, but ahead of you on the trail.

"We'd have had a hard time of it without him," Immanuel said, still looking in the direction the Injun had traveled.

"That's spoken truth if it was ever," Uzziah agreed, and he took the folded-up paper and unfolded it. "What do you know!" he exclaimed.

Immanuel looked over. "I know a lot, old son."

"Look at that," Uzziah said, and he turned the sheet of paper toward Immanuel.

"Damn! It's like he's looking right out at ya!"

"My mother draws."

"She drew that!?!"

"Reckon so, otherwise how would Abooksigun have had it on him?"

"Well," Immanuel said, as he opened up his big saddlebags. "We's a puttin' that away so it'll stay nice. We can hang it up in the cabins," he said as he took the drawing, folded it once, and placed it in there where there was another sheet of the identical paper, already folded.

"What's that?" Uzziah asked.

"What's what?" Immanuel said, shutting the saddlebag and trying to play innocent.

"That other piece of paper right next to the drawing of Abooksigun."

"Oh, that?"

"Yeah, that."

"It ain't noithin', truly."

"Show it to me," Uzziah said, scooting his big black horse, Shadow, closer to Trevor, Immanuel's horse.

Immanuel started to reach in the saddlebag, then stopped. "It's just gonna make ya unhappy," he said, "and ya know how much I wants ya to be happy, right?

"Wagh!" Uzziah yelled in Immanuel's face.

"Wagh!" Immanuel yelled right back.

They both sat there grinning at each other, then Uzziah spoke up.

"How could a piece of paper make me unhappy, old son?"

"It could, it just could, I knows it."

"Show me the damned drawing," Uzziah demanded.

Immanuel handed Uzziah the piece of paper. He unfolded it, and there was Abooksigun looking back at him.

"The other one!"

"How ya know it's a drawing? It could be plans fer a new cabin, an outhouse design yer pa showed me."

"Show it to me!"

"Okay, okay, okay," Immanuel said and took the piece of paper out like it was a sacred artifact.

Immanuel unfolded it and admired what he saw.

Uzziah snatched for it, but Immanuel was quick for an older man.

"Give it! Uzziah shouted, and his voice echoed off the hills. "Give it, give it, give it..."

Immanuel smiled. "It's gonna make ya hate me, I knows it is."

"Well, ya not showing me has already helped me to a strong dislike fer ya, so go on, and get it over with!"

Immanuel James Jones turned the drawing around, and Uzziah nearly fell off his horse.

"What in God's name!" Uzziah looked away to save his eyes, then managed to bring his vision back around to gaze at the drawing, then, he swore an oath.

"I weren't really nakedie nude, I was dressed, she just imagined the rest," Jones said.

"Uh, huh," Uzziah said, snatching it away from Immanuel.

"Be careful, be careful!"

"So, yer worried I might crumple it up and use it to start a fire, is that it?

"Come on, now, ya wouldn't do that—would ya!?!"

Uzziah acted like he was going to do just that, and when Immanuel drew a deep breath, Uzziah stopped.

"So, my mother, Rahab O'Bannon, just happened to imagine that lance scar down there in yer nether regions right over yer Johnson? Is that what yer lyin' to me about?"

"It was innocent as hell—"

"Where were ya?" Uzziah asked.

"In her studio—"

"In the attic?"

Immanuel just nodded his head up and down, then added, "Well, ya know how hot it is up there."

"Hot enough fer ya to strip off everything, I do mean everything, but yer hat? Why did ya leave yer hat on?"

"She asked me to," he said apologetically.

"So, she didn't mind ya taking off ever' dern thin' ya had on, but she asked ya to leave on yer hat, is that it?"

"She asked me to leave on the hat, partner, I swear, said it said a lot about me personality."

Uzziah swung the Hawken that laid across the pommel of the saddle in Immanuel's direction.

"Nothin' happened, nothin'!"

"Did she take off her clothes?" Uzziah asked.

"What kinda woman would that make her?" Immanuel seemed insulted for Rahab O'Bannon.

"Did she?!" Uzziah said, cocking the Hawken.

"No! Absolutely not! She was sweating like a pig, now I didn't mean anything bad by that, she was simply perspiring like a lady, but it was a lot of perspiration, I tell ya."

"Ma Rahab can sweat, that's fer sure," Uzziah said, remembering her working in the fields with all the boys and handling her weight as if she were a man, and she sweated like one.

"It's only natchual for a hard workin' woman," Immanuel wanted to agree wherever there was a chance.

"Don't mine me sayin' so, partner," Uzziah said,

looking at the picture held up with one hand, and keeping the other hand on the Hawken. "Yer member looks a might engorged!"

"Does it? Let me see."

Uzziah kept the drawing away from Immanuel. "Take it from me, old son, it certainly ain't no spider on a stove, ifn ya get my drift."

"Well, it was hot up there, and I ain't never been ogled by a woman—"

"Yer sayin' my godly mother ogled yer Johnson?!" Uzziah put his finger on the trigger.

"Well, how do ya think she got all them fine details, down to the hairs of the pubic variety?"

Uzziah couldn't keep it in any longer, he bent over and started laughing as he handed back the drawing.

"Ya done lost yer mind, ain't ya?" Immanuel asked. "And it's all my fault!"

"Nah, partner, my ma done drew every one of her children in the buff, and Pa, too, and she had him keep his hat on," he said, chuckling the whole time.

"So," Immanuel said, folding the drawing and putting it back in the saddlebag beside the one of Abooksigun. "She done drew the girls naked?" he asked, wiping the saliva from his lips.

Uzziah raised the Hawken again. "Now who's a nosy Parker!?!"

"How old were they when she drew 'em?"

"She does it every year. She drew me in the nude while we was there, too, fool," Uzziah said.

Immanuel was trying not to imagine Sarah, Sally, and little innocent Faith lying up there on the same mattress he'd propped himself up on. He had to say something to cover his prurient nature, so he blurted out, "Ya got a strange family, young son."

"Watch it—"

"Strange and wonderful, I mean, strange and wonderful that's fer sure," Immanuel said, trying to imagine what Sarah and the other women in the family looked like naked. His Johnson was beginning to respond to his very active imagination.

"Yer thoughts are in the outhouse hole, so just stop it right now," Uzziah warned.

Immanuel looked at Uzziah and smiled.

"What's up now, besides yer Johnson?" Uzziah asked, looking at the bulge in Immanuel's pants.

Immanuel covered the bulge with his Hawken. "Sometimes, I think yer a pervert."

"Right back at ya, old son," Uzziah said. "So where to now?"

"Let's drop by Vrain's and get whiskey, tobaccy, and sundries, what ya say?"

"Hey, I ain't got a job, I'm free as a damn bird," Uzziah said, and he kicked Shadow up into a trot toward the trading post.

———

They rode without talking, and that's what friends, true friends, can do, not talk just to be filling the void between them. True friends know that there is a sacred space where we think our thoughts and they can think theirs, and to each belong the privacy of those thoughts, and the giving away of those thoughts constitutes a lessening of who we are. Keeping your thoughts to yourself is what these mountain men did.

When they talked, they talked, but when they didn't, their thoughts were their own, as their eyes surveyed the surrounding hills, the creek beds, and any place that someone might be hiding, ready to take them away from not only their thoughts but their very existence.

They rode into the trading post at Vrain in the early afternoon. The sun was still a bit hot, and the cloud cover was spotty, which gave them some relief, like it did at that very moment as the golden orb slipped behind some nimbostratus piling up in the north. It may rain later in the day, and that would have been fine by both mountain men.

Several ponies were tied up out front, and they were just that, ponies with fine horse war bridles on them, the kind comprised of a loop that encircles the horse's lower jaw, resting in the same area in which a normal White man's bridle would rest. It stays in the mouth because it is snug, not tight around the lower jaw, the ends of which are in the hands of the riders. The blankets were nice-looking, and Immanuel recognized the weaving as the work of the Crow Nation. So, he guessed correctly that five Crows were in there trading their wares.

There was another set of horses, almost like someone had put them there just for contrast. They were underfed, uncombed, and mangy-looking with torn-up saddles, and the reins had broken on them in several places, but instead of replacing them, they had simply tied the broken ends together in a square knot. Some of the horses were missing shoes, and a couple of these five horses had feet that were way too long. Both Immanuel and Uzziah just shook their heads as they tied their mounts up away from those flea-bitten creatures, and next to the Injun ponies.

When they walked in and their eyes had adjusted to the darkness compared to the brilliant light from the sun, the men who owned those poorly cared for horses could be smelled before they were seen. They were huddled together in the back of the store and whispering about something. Uzziah looked over and there were four of the most beautiful Crow women he'd ever seen, and he supposed the mangy cowboys were whispering about them, who knew?

There was a man at the counter. He had broad shoulders and longish curly black hair that jutted out from under what some people called a buckaroo sombrero. He was clad for riding, and his dark jacket was in good shape, but you could tell he'd had it for a while. He was buying something and his back was turned toward the front door, but the manner in which those Crow squaws were standing around him, really in sort of a half circle, it was obvious to Uzziah and Immanuel that they weren't just standing there, they had the man's back and that was that.

Well, the two mountain men went to the second counter, separated by a pile of goods, and hailed one of the other men to wait on them. The tobacco and whiskey weren't out in the open, you had to ask for it. They were getting their supplies of both when loud voices broke out near the Crow women and the man who was with them.

"I said them is the bestest lookin' nigger squaws I ever seen, that's exactly what I said," the obvious leader of the mangy saddle tramps said. The man at the counter still hadn't turned around, but after that last comment, he did so very slowly.

"Hell," Immanuel whispered to Uzziah, "that's James Beckwourth!"

"Who?" Uzziah whispered back.

"Shut up and just watch," Immanuel said.

"Were you referring to my four wives, gentlemen?" Beckwourth asked the man who had a beard that looked like a growth on his face.

"Well, well, ifn the nigger squaws ain't got themselves a real nigger husband!"

"If you want to insult me, yer gonna hafta do better than that, gents. I mean I've pretty much heard it all, so give it yer best shot, okay?" Beckwourth said, putting his thumbs in his vest where the arm holes were. He was wearing low-slung Griswolds on his left and right hips, and his hands were nowhere near the guns.

"Well, how about this, we's gonna fuck all them nigger squaws before the day is through," the man said, looking at the women, then back at his so-called men who were giggling like ugly girls at a barn dance.

"You see, that attempt to insult them was lost. They don't speak yer filthy language, they only speak Crow."

"Caw, caw!" the bad beard man screamed, then added, "Then, why don't ya translate that fer 'em, huh?"

Beckwourth spoke in perfect Crow to the women who listened intently, and then laughed like hyenas as they spoke back to Beckwourth in Crow.

"What'd ya say to 'em?!?" the man demanded, his partners were getting itchy for the fight they knew was coming. They'd pulled back their disgusting, greasy jackets, exposing their not-well-maintained firearms.

"I told them exactly what you said, but left out them being niggers. They said, if you tried to do anything like that, they would make tobacco pouches out of yer scrotums."

The leader looked at the other four, who shrugged.

"What the hell's a scro-tum?" he asked, curious to know.

"Yer ball sacks, that is, if ya got any?" Beckwourth said, not cracking a smile.

Several of the mangy saddle tramps actually put their hands over their private parts.

"Take 'em boys!" the leader yelled and went for his gun.

The other four drew, and two went down by the butts of Hawken rifles, and the other two had the cocked Hawkens thrusted into their backs.

The man who had drawn on Beckwourth had his wrist broken by Beckwourth, who drew lightning fast and cracked the barrel of the Griswold over the man's wrist, his pistola hitting the dirt floor of the trading post.

"Ya broke my damn wrist!" he howled and Beckwourth leveled a left hook into his face, his head snapped around, bloody spital flying from it as he went down unconscious.

The others grabbed their unconscious leader, and they all went out of the trading post.

The four Crow women were standing there with long knives drawn and no expression on their faces.

Beckwourth looked at Immanuel. "I know you, don't I, sir?"

"I am amazed and honored that ya would 'member, sir," Immanuel said. "This is my partner Uzziah

Ferguson O'Bannon. Uzziah, this is James Pierson Beckwourth."

Uzziah shook Beckwourth's hand as he turned to Immanuel. "You, sir, have a prodigious memory, and where was it that we met, for I do not remember."

"It was at Rendezvous many years ago," Immanuel said.

"Yes, yes, I remember now, back in my trapping days. Didn't you have that Mandan wife—"

"She has since passed," Immanuel said, not wanting her name repeated.

"Then I shall not say her name, she was beautiful and I could see that she loved Immanuel James Jones very much," Beckwourth said, extending his hand, and the two men did that thing that Uzziah himself did, but still did not understand.

"Wagh!!" they both shouted into each other's faces, then the four Crow women ululated, making that wonderful sound with their tongues.

Beckwourth turned to them, and in Crow, spoke for a long time. Then turned to the two mountain men.

"They are grateful for braves who do not fear acting, and wish you both many smokes from your teepees."

Both Uzziah and Immanuel bowed to the women, though neither of them had ever done such a thing. The Crow women loved it and ululated some more.

"Well, we have what we came fer and have a distance to go before we camp," Beckwourth said.

"Pleasure was all ours, sir," Uzziah said.

"I detect a Virginian accent in you, Irish."

"Shenandoah Valley near Laurel," Uzziah said.

"I was born at the mouth of the Shenandoah Valley

up north," Beckwourth said. "Ever so glad to meet a fellow Virginian."

"Likewise," Uzziah said.

"Well, wish we had time to visit, but our journey calls us away," Beckwourth said and then spoke to the Crow women who left in front of him.

When the men got outside, the Crow women had taken the liberty of handing their reins to the two mountain men. They handed Shadow's reins to Uzziah and Trevor's reins to Immanuel, neither of them thought anything about it at the time. They waited for the men to mount up, then jumped onto their ponies, two in front and two behind Beckwourth, a sort of squaw patrol of protection for Beckwourth.

"May the wind be at your back," Beckwourth said.

Uzziah followed with, "And the road rise up to meet you." Then, the five of them went south.

Uzziah and Immanuel sat their respective horses and watched them leave.

"We're doin' a lot of this watchin' folks leave, ain't we?" Immanuel remarked.

"He remembered yer name, old son," Uzziah commented.

"And the Crow women handed the right reins to the right man, did ya catch that?"

"How in hell?" Uzziah queried.

"They know their horses, and they know their men," Immanuel said, then looking around said, "Where'd the trail trash get to?"

Uzziah just shrugged.

"Let's go up into the foothills and see what's shakin'," Immanuel said as he kicked up Trevor.

The two men rode for twenty minutes into the hills

surrounding the Vrain Trading Post, and Immanuel pulled the spyglass from his saddlebags. He opened her up and spied the trails north and south.

"What ya see?" Uzziah asked.

"Nothin'—wait, wait, there the scum is, they're trailing Beckwourth and his wives. Come on, let's see where the trash will be blown," Immanuel said, handing the glass to Uzziah, who took his look, folded up the glass, and handed it back to Immanuel as they dog trotted off into the foothills parallel to the trail going south.

They kept off the crests of the hills and followed along the hills. They were on them all day, until the sun was setting. Immanuel glassed them again. "Beckwourth's setting up camp. Well, his wives are, and the trail trash has stopped short of them. They're waiting until night to jump 'em," Immanuel said as they rode down in the general direction of Beckwourth's camp.

2

They could actually smell the trail trash before they spotted their cold camp. At least they had the sense not to build a fire with four Crow women up ahead. Immanuel and Uzziah figured their plan of revenge was simple, they'd wait 'til early morning when most folks are fast asleep and go in, kill Beckwourth, and rape his Crow wives.

Uzziah and Immanuel went to either side of the camp where James was staying with the four Crow women. They stayed far enough away and made sure they were downwind at all times. They were there to help, and showing up before trouble started wouldn't have done anyone any good at all. They ate jerked meat and drank from streams in the area. They planned to come to the aid of the five travelers when things went south. At the first sign of trouble, shots, raised voices, or anything like that, they would come in from the sides, a sort of pinching movement which would allow them the luxury of taking the men without them knowing what was happening.

Uzziah had intended to stay awake, but he was tired and ready to be back at the cabins, which they would have been if it hadn't been for this protective detail. When he heard a shot, he jumped on Shadow and rode toward the sound of fighting.

When he got there, Immanuel was coming into the camp from the opposite side. The four Crow women had their long knives out, and the boys who had eyes on them earlier were cut up a bit. They had fired one shot, and it looked like Beckwourth was lying beside the fire. They didn't know if he was alive or dead. They had expected the Crow women to be easier prey, but by the looks of their cut-up arms and stomachs, it wasn't working out that way.

"All right, it's over!" Immanuel said, pointing the Hawken into the firelight.

"He's only one, boys, and he's got to reload before he can take another shot, take him and let's get this quim saddled up and follerin' us," the man with the wrapped wrist shouted at his men. He had barely finished that statement when his head was shot through and through with the big slug from one of the Hawkens. Most of his brain ended up on his men, who lost just enough time being repulsed in horror to allow what happened next.

Recovering, one of the others started to shoot Immanuel when his heart was blown through his chest. He stood there looking at the hole before he slumped to his knees in the dirt.

A tomahawk was thrown by Immanuel. He had had Abooksigun teach him how to throw one, and it hit the one in the back who turned toward Uzziah. His legs were rubber as he fell and started screaming, "My legs are gone, my legs are gone!"

The fourth man was about to shoot Immanuel when Uzziah's Bowie knife lodged in his throat and blood shot out three feet from where he was standing. He reached up, managed to pull Uzziah's knife out, and bled out in less than a minute.

The last of the men saw good sense, and ran for his horse, but halfway there, four knives were thrown by the Crow women and he was a pincushion on the run 'til he hit a Ponderosa and fell backward hitting the dirt, driving each of the tips of the knives through his chest, sticking out his shirt.

Immanuel walked over to take a look at Beckwourth, and on the way, nonchalantly shot the man who was screaming about his legs in the head. He bounced up a little and was gone, not worrying any more about his pains.

All four Crows were around Beckwourth, and when Uzziah got there, they had bandaged his head up, but Immanuel made them unwrap the wound so he could look at it. He got some herbs from his saddlebags, and crushing them in his hands, he applied them to the graze wound that had cut a trough through the left side of the wounded man's head, then the Crow women, nodding in approval, wound the bandages back around Beckwourth's head. He was unconscious but still looked like a formidable foe. Two of the Crow women cut limbs from nearby trees and made a travois, and Immanuel gathered the poor horses that had been treated so badly by the five men. He shot the mangiest one, who looked close to death anyway, tied the other four tail-to-chin, and the first one to his horse, Trevor, who looked around as if to say, *What!*

The travois was finished and bows of freshly cut Ponderosa pines were placed on it, covered by blankets. James Beckwourth, the famous mountain man, trapper, Crow war chief, and husband of four Crow women, was loaded upon the travois.

Immanuel spoke to the women in sign language, which seemed to be universal among the nations. Uzziah was getting better at that language, and he could tell that Immanuel was telling them that their mutual husband would be taken to our cabins, and that it was his sacred duty to see to the Crow women's safety. They looked at him, then had a short conversation about it, then mounted up and told him in sign that he should lead on!

———

The first night out, which wasn't that far away in hours, saw them camped by a stream and the four Crow women tending to Beckwourth. He moaned a lot and said some things in the middle of the night that scared even Immanuel James Jones.

"Cut off the fucking White man's heads and piss down their throats!" Beckwourth yelled loudly, then went back to his coma.

Uzziah looked over at Immanuel in his bedroll and he was rubbing his neck.

Several hours later, he said clear as a bell, "Ifn ya want me dead, kill me, otherwise I will live with you." Uzziah learned later that was what Immanuel had always heard Beckwourth had said when he rode into a hostile Crow camp one wintery night in the Montana territory.

It took them about a day and a half to get to the cabins. When they stopped for water and to eat jerky, Immanuel would put another poultice on Beckwourth's head and rewrap the bandages. The Crow women were concerned about one thing and one thing only, their half White, half Black husband. Uzziah had seen mulatos before, and it was obvious to him that Beckwourth's birth had been the White master who was interested in one of his female slaves, a common occurrence in Virginia at the time.

The Crow women carried their husband into the biggest of the cabins, telling Immanuel in sign that they would take that cabin to nurse the man back to health. Immanuel was fine with that, but confided in Uzziah around the fire that night.

"They think he'll recover, and maybe he will, but head wounds are weird," Immanuel said.

"How you mean?"

"He might not be the same man when he wakes up,' Immanuel said, lighting his pipe with a burning stick from the fire.

"Not the same man?"

"Yeah, he might be somebody else," Immanuel said.

"How could that happen?"

"Don't ask me, I seen it, I didn't cause it."

———

They decided to sleep in different cabins just in case

the Crows decided that they wanted to kill the White man who had saved them.

"Why would they kill us?" Uzziah asked in disbelief.

"I always told ya straight, Injuns are notional, and these Crow women ain't any different. They might just decide it was our interference at the trading post that got those others roweled up. Our deaths might not make any sense to us, but what does that matter, they're four of them and only two of us."

They slept like that until early morning, when they heard a scream, and when both of them ran from their separate cabins, all they saw were the shirttails of James Beckwourth flying out behind him as he ran away down the hill. It was not winter, and that was good. All that might happen to him was a bear, or a mountain lion, or maybe he'd run off a cliff, he didn't know the area.

"Why'd he run like that?" Uzziah asked.

"That ain't Beckwourth," Immanuel said.

"A different man?" Uzziah asked, and Immanuel nodded his head up and down,

All this time, four Crow women were frantically talking to them. Immanuel started signing and they said they wanted to go after him. Immanuel told them to go ahead, that he was waiting for daylight in order to track him, no one's going out in the night. They agreed, then left immediately to find him.

"What'd I tell ya, notional. They agreed to wait fer sunup, then left in the middle of the night."

Uzziah and Immanuel looked at each other.

"Guess we'd better join 'em, huh?" Uzziah asked.

"Hell no! It's dark, partner, dark, there ain't even a

moon. I am staying right chere by the fire while they stumble around in the dark. Chances are we'll be fixing broken legs and arms before the morning comes."

"But they're women out there in the dark!" Uzziah protested.

"No, they are Injun women, Crow women out there in the dark, and ifn ya stumbled into one of 'em they're just as likely to stick ya with one of their long knives as smile, and that young son, is the truth."

———

Meanwhile, Beckwourth was running from the slave plantation where they treated him like what he was—a slave! He felt his head and realized that one of the masters must have gotten fed up with his sass and tried to shoot him. He'd only been grazed in the head, and that was his luck and his God coming in for him. His feet were bare, and the limbs and rocks were cutting them up something awful, but he could hear the hounds behind him in the brush. He dared not stop or he would no longer be free.

The pains he was going through—the cutting up of his feet and the turning of his ankles on rocks—that suffering was nothing compared to the fact of being owned by someone. He found a stream, and drank deeply. The water tasted better than any water ever had, it was, after all, free-man's water! The hounds were crashing through the woods again, and their howling sounded rather odd, but maybe the master had bought new dogs.

He knew the master had laid with his mammy plenty of times, and maybe they was going to have some more kids and now he was dispensable, who knew with these crazy cracker whites! He was not going to be caught this time, not this time. He found a cave to hide in, and as he got inside, he heard the sound of growling. Shit, a bear was in there, well, he was going to have to kick the bear out, he ran out and grabbed a hefty limb and went in and started beating the bear over the head.

The bear was surprised to be awakened and he had done his best growl, but this dark man, this villain, had just left, gotten a big stick, come back in, and started bear-beating him. He would have to kill the dark man.

Several times, Beckwourth's torso was swiped by the bear's claws, but each time that happened, the man stabbed at the face of the bear with the long club. The bear howled in pain as one of his eyes was poked out. The bear decided to leave, the dark man could have the cave, he'd find another one and lick his wounds there.

Beckwourth was satisfied that the cave was now his, but he kept the long limb he'd used to fight the bear nearby as he fell into a deep sleep.

———

Daylight was welcomed by the two mountain men. The four Crow women had come back without a single scratch on them. Immanuel was impressed. He signed for them to get some sleep while he and Uzziah went looking for their husband, or whomever he thought he was at this point in his dementia.

Finding the trail wasn't a problem. The man had trampled everything in his way to escape, because escaping was the only thing that made sense to him.

"He was a slave before his pa freed him. His ma was

just a negress and he had eyes for her evidently and she, him," Immanuel said as they rode along easily following the beaten trail the man had left behind in his frenzy to escape captivity. Immanuel noticed there was blood on the trail, the man had, after all, left without his boots.

"How do ya know all this?" Uzziah asked.

"At that rendezvous, when I met him, it was about the only thing that was spoken about. I'm tellin' ya the man is a legend in his own time, no jokin'. And that legend wasn't the man who ran from the cabins last night."

"Then who'd he supposes he thought he was?"

"He certainly wasn't James Beckwourth the tracker, Injun guide, or trapper when he ran. My best guess is, he's gone back in time—"

"Sometimes, you are so full of hooey, I swear!"

"I am, am I?"

"Yeah."

"'Member that Pinkerton Agent?"

"Yeah, ole Robert Spells, weren't it?"

"Sure 'nough, he could spell, but he didn't cipher north from south, talk about a tenderfoot!"

"What about him?" Uzziah asked.

"'Member when he lost hisself and he just went off with the old man?"

"Yeah."

"Well, he weren't old enough to go back too far, that's why he was so pliable, but this chere Beckwourth has lived a long time in this world. And what was he in the beginning?"

"How in the hell should I know!?!" Uzziah objected.

"He were a slave, young son."

"Yeah, ya told me that," Uzziah said.

"Well, you tell me, what does a slave do first chance he gets?"

"Run."

"Now, yer gettin' smart. That nigger woke up in that dark cabin with only the fire for light, and when he saw he was alone, and unchained, well, he just lit on outta there!" Immanuel said as if he'd solved something.

"How does that help us find him?" Uzziah went right to the point.

"Findin' him is a cinch, figurin' out how to treat him, now, that's the problem."

"What ya mean?"

"Who are we gonna look like from his slaved past?"

"How the hell should I know!" Uzziah was getting fed up with all this conjecturing.

"No, wait!"

"Fer what?"

"Lookie yonder," Immanuel whispered.

When Uzziah looked, he had to search through the branches of some ponderosas, and a lot of deadfall, but there he was, not a hundred yards away, drinking from a stream. It was definitely James Beckwourth, and his head was on a swivel as he was looking for somebody. Unfortunately for him, his head was also still bandaged in light colored cloth—you could spot him a mile away.

Immanuel edged Trevor over beside Shadow. "He's gonna think we're slave catchers."

Uzziah looked at Immanuel like he'd lost his cork and all the liquid had flowed out.

Immanuel got his rope out and handed it to Uzziah, who refused it and got his own. He was used to

173

throwing his, and he'd spent hour after hour some afternoons throwing at a stump like it was a cow.

Immanuel leaned over and whispered in Uzziah's ear,,"This chere stump is gonna be runnin'," he said and he nodded forward as he eased Trevor forward with Uzziah right behind him. When they got about fifty yards from Beckwourth, they were still blocked basically by all the underbrush, but Immanuel thought he'd try something first.

"James Pierson Beckwourth!" he yelled, and the man at the stream who was washing off his face now and putting water on his side, looked up and immediately took the stance of someone getting ready to run. "Yer pa set ya free, son, yer no longer a slave! Remember?"

Beckwourth was on the run and he was running down the middle of the stream, slipping on rocks and Uzziah had Shadow galloping up right behind him, water splashing all around, not making it exactly easy to see the running cow, and when the man looked around, the look on his face was sheer terror. Uzziah just threw the rope once, and all that practicing came true, it slipped around the man, and when Shadow was called to whoa, Beckwourth went off his feet and down in the stream with a great splash!

He was fighting like a madman, trying to get the rope off himself, but Uzziah had.

Shadow stepping backward and dragging Beckwourth upstream. Immanuel rode up and jumped off Trevor and onto Beckwourth and it was like two cats fighting. They tumbled in the stream, but Beckwourth had his arms almost tied to his body, and it wasn't much of a fight. Finally, amid shouts of, "You ain't takin' me back! You ain't!" Immanuel had the man tied up and dragged him out of the stream. Both men were soaking wet and heaving as if they might not catch their breaths.

"Ever do any bulldoggin'?" Uzziah asked.

"What the hell is bulldoggin'?"

"Guess that means, ya ain't," Uzziah said, sorry he'd brought it up.

Beckwourth's eyes were as big as saucers, and he was trembling, either from the cold stream or fear. He got down on his knees and begged, "Please, massa, please, please, don't take me back, massa!"

"Stop talkin'," was all Immanuel said, and the mulato man shut his mouth. "Do you know who we are?" Immanuel asked him

"You're slave hunters, slave catchers sent after me by my owner," Beckwourth said.

"No, we ain't!"

Beckwourth looked between the two men and shook his head. "Then who is ya?"

"Believe it or not, we're yer friends," Immanuel said.

"The devil is being nice so's I's believe him," Beckwourth said.

Uzziah looked at Immanuel and shook his head no, then spoke, "Yer right, we're gonna get a handsome sum fer yer black ass, I can tell ya."

"Now there's a man who speaks truth," the mulato said.

Immanuel just looked at Uzziah as if he'd spoiled all his work.

"And we will beat the livin' shite out of ya, ifn ya try to run again, ya got that, boy!"

Immanuel was just looking at Uzziah as if he'd lost his mind. Uzziah rode over close to where Immanuel was standing, dripping wet. "Ya said it yerself, he's back in Virginny and a slave, ain't no good in tryin' nothin' else but what he thinks he knows 'til he comes around."

Immanuel just shrugged as if to say, give it yer best shot!

"These woods don't look like Virginia, do they?" Uzziah asked the mulato.

Beckwourth looked around and there seemed to be something dawning in his brain.

"I musta run a whole long way," he said, smiling.

"Well, these here mountains are two thousand miles from Virginny, ya think ya ran that damn far?" Uzziah asked him.

"This must be part of the Smokies I ain't never seen," Beckwourth said, trying to reconcile what he knew from his past in the mountains and the way these mountains looked.

"Well, we'll beat ya, like I said, ifn ya don't come peaceful-like, there's some people who want to see ya," Immanuel said, getting into the act.

"Yes, boss," Beckwourth said, and he got to his feet as best he could. "Ya ride and I'll walk."

"Damn straight, y'all walk," Immanuel said.

———

It wasn't that far back to the cabins, and when the four Crow women saw how they had brought back Beckwourth, they had their knives out and they were chattering away in Crow to the Black man.

"What they want, and who is they? What they mumbling on about?" Beckwourth said.

"You can't understand 'em?" Uzziah asked the man.

"They's the three witches from Macbeth, ain't they?"

Immanuel looked to Uzziah and both men realized that Beckwourth had known how to read when he was a young man, and still a slave, and not just a simple book, but the Bard!

"This chere play is more like King Lear," Uzziah said, and Immanuel wondered where this was going.

"They's my daughters?" Beckwourth asked.

"Not exactly," Immanuel said.

"Then who is they?!" Beckwourth asked as one of them came up and speaking Crow sweetly, she stroked his face, and kissed him on the cheek.

"They is my daughters, this is King Lear," Beckwourth said, then added, "Which one is she?"

"Ya don't recognize Cordelia, yer favorite daughter?" Immanuel asked.

"She's my youngest," Beckwourth said, and gave her a kiss on the forehead.

"We can't let him go on with this, all three are dead in the end and he goes insane," Uzziah whispered to Immanuel.

"Maybe he'll just come around?" Immanuel said hopefully.

"Hey, you two slave catchers!" Beckwourth shouted, and it scared the wife he had been thinking was Cordelia and she backed away.

"Yeah?" Immanuel said.

"How can a slave be King?"

"Ya got us there," Uzziah said.

"How can bottom rung be top rung!?!"

"As I said, that's a sure 'nough quandary, Beckwourth," Immanuel said.

"That my name?"

"One of 'em," Immanuel said.

"What's the rest of 'em?" Beckwourth asked.

"James Pierson Beckwourth," Immanuel said.

"That's a good name, but I don't recognize it," he said, touching the side of his head where the bullet had grazed him.

The four Crow women were signing to Immanuel, and he watched for a bit, then said, "They's gonna fix ya up a bit. I see yer side is bleedin' and yer head was hurt by a bullet."

"The bear wanted his cave, we fought, but I knowed ya shot me, didn't ya!?"

"He fought a bear for a cave?" Uzziah whispered to Immanuel, who just shrugged.

"It weren't us, James," Uzziah said, "twas others who wanted to do ya harm."

"Likely story, White man."

"It's the onliest story we got," Immanuel said, then added, "Can they, yer daughters, put ya back together, King Lear?"

"Sure, they seem nice enough," Beckwourth said.

The Crow women spent about an hour nursing his wounds and putting poultices on them that Immanuel had the herbs for. They were gentle with him and seemed to understand that the bullet, which almost went into his head, did the damage it did by just passing by and making the groove. They continued to talk to him in Crow and Uzziah and Immanuel thought that just might be the right thing, maybe that foreign language which he had learned would bring him around.

Old King Lear was tired after that, and he went to

sleep in Cordelia's lap. Uzziah and Immanuel could see that the other Crow wives were jealous. They sat around and kept looking at the one with their husband's head in her lap like she had committed some crime. Eventually, she traded places with them, and then everybody seemed happy.

3

Immanuel and Uzziah were worried about James Beckwourth. They knew who he was, his four Crow wives knew who he was, but he had not a clue. The Crow women had put him to bed, and Immanuel spent a great deal of time around the campfire signing what he thought had happened to the man. Luckily, two of his four wives had remembered a similar case in their village. On a buffalo hunt, a brave had fallen from his pony and been badly trampled. When his wounds were fixed, he had no idea what had happened to him, and the medicine man in the village had said that now, this brave had stronger medicine than anyone in the village, but suddenly his memories did return and the woman who had taken him in was greatly relieved to have her husband back. He went on to live the rest of his life normally, not bothered by memory problems again.

It was while they were talking that one of the Crow women went into the cabin which Beckwourth had run from as if he were a captive, and she came out with a leather satchel. She handed it to Immanuel, telling him that Beckwourth spent many hours every week making tracks in the books inside the satchel. She handed him the satchel, hoping that it would help.

That night, after the Crow women had gone to sleep and they had decided that one of them should stand guard, Immanuel took the first shift.

When he opened the satchel out of boredom and realized that Beckwourth had chronicled his entire life since he had been set free, it seemed to present a solution of sorts. Everything was in there, all his adventures, and just about every man he'd had to kill—the tale was told why he had to, and how it had been done. Immanuel wondered why any man would write down the people he had killed, but decided later that Beckwourth had a strong feeling for human life, since he'd seen it so sorely abused when he was a slave.

By the time it was Uzziah's turn to take guard duty over the famous man, Immanuel was still wide awake.

"He's got his whole life right here. He recorded everything, even some things that could probably get him arrested if anyone wanted him to be," Immanuel said.

"Let me see," Uzziah asked and was handed the first journal while Immanuel picked the second leather-bound journal. They sat and read in the firelight, neither of them wanting to put the journals down.

By the time morning had come, Immanuel had fallen asleep beside the fire, and Uzziah had covered him with a blanket. Uzziah could read faster than his partner, and when the Crow women emerged from their cabin, and Beckwourth walked out, he seemed different in some way.

"You okay?" Uzziah asked Beckwourth.

"Yes," he said, and then grabbed a tin cup and poured black coffee into it.

"Something's different about you," Uzziah noted as Beckwourth sipped the hot, black coffee.

"These women," he whispered to Uzziah, "I do not know them, but each of them came to me in the night and offered me what only a husband should be offered." He finished up and looked sideways at the women who were cooking breakfast.

"That's a'cause yer their husband, fool!" Uzziah whispered back, trying to keep it confidential, the way Beckwourth seemed to want it.

Beckwourth took the news stoically. He sipped the coffee and looked at the women, then sipped some more. Finally, he spoke. "Am I a Mormon?"

Uzziah belted out a laugh that scared the Crow women and woke up Immanuel.

Beckwourth, seeing how bleary-eyed Immanuel was and how startled the Crow women were, started laughing, too.

Immanuel sat up, and one of the Crow women handed him coffee, and he signed his thanks.

"I'd forgotten about laughter," Beckwourth said, making the hand sign for laughter by moving both hands, palms up alternately in an up and down manner.

The women signed to him, and he signed back.

"I don't know how I'm doing this, but I understand all these hand movements?" Beckwourth said.

"It's called sign by the natives, and ya sure do know it, Beckwourth," Immanuel said, trying to continue to reinforce the man's name every chance he could.

"It feels good, don't it?" Uzziah commented about

the laughter, and Uzziah made the signing for laughter. He made a promise to himself to learn this hand language.

"Yes, yes, it does. My chest feels liberated," Beckwourth said.

"That's a good way to look at laughter," Uzziah said, smiling, then added, "Next time I laugh, I'll remember that."

"Hey, I been reading your journals," Immanuel said.

"My what?"

"You kept a fairly good account of what's been going on in yer life since ya got yer freedom from yer pa," Immanuel said. "And it's all in here," he said and raised up the satchel.

"Really?"

"Yeah," Uzziah said, "and you ain't half bad at drawing neither."

"Let me see them," Beckwourth asked.

Uzziah handed the satchel to him, and he took one of the journals and looked inside.

"I like the pictures," he said, and Immanuel's heart sank. He had wondered about the ability for Beckwourth to read, and now, he imagined he had his answer.

"What about the words?" Immanuel asked.

"Those tracks on the pages, that's what they're called?"

"Yes, sir, ya can't read them though, can ya?"

"No, they look like the trails of snails as they slowly glide across a big leaf, but do they mean more than that?"

"Oh yes, yes sir, they do," Uzziah offered.

After they ate breakfast, they made up a plan. Uzziah and Immanuel would sit beside the man called Beckwourth and read his journals to him. There were about twenty-four of them, and besides the few drawings here and there, it was all writing. The good news was, Beckwourth had an impeccable hand at script, and they wouldn't be that hard to read.

They started that very day with Immanuel reading and Beckwourth sitting by the fire and listening. Sometimes he would laugh, sometimes what was written when read would make him cry, but he seemed thoroughly entranced by the stories of what he thought was another man's life.

"This man who wrote these things, he was careless in his doing so, yes?" Beckwourth asked.

"Perhaps, what do'ya mean?"

"These killings, especially of the White men, even if they were bad hombres, he could be hung in Virginny for those, couldn't he?"

"He sure could," Uzziah said from the other side of the cabin. He was sitting by the open door with the sunlight spilling across his lap. He was whittling a horse.

"I think I can do that," Beckwourth said.

"Whittle?" Uzziah asked.

"Is that what's called?"

"Yes. Whittling with a sharp knife, not exactly something ya want a kid to do."

"I think I made toys like that for children who looked like the ladies who say they are my wives," Beckwourth said.

"Well, hell," Immanuel said, "maybe we're gettin' somewhere!"

Early on that same morning, eleven fellas walked into the Vrain Trading Post. They had a similar smell and all-out nasty look about them as the five who had followed Beckwourth and his four Crow wives.

"Can I be of assistance to you gentlemen?" the proprietor, Jean Baptiste, asked in a strong French accent.

"Maybe ya can, maybe ya can't," the man who seemed to be in charge of the other ten said.

"Do you wish to buy liquor or tobacco?"

"Yeah, probably, but I gots a question fer ya."

"*Si vous plait?*" the Frenchman behind the counter said, and then, seeing that they did not possess the knowledge of French, translated for them. "Certainly, ask away," he said.

"Did about five fellas come through here not long ago?"

"We have many people who come through, can you be less general?"

"Yeah, one of 'em was my twin brother, so did you see me pass through?"

The man at the other counter spoke in rapid French to the man who was waiting on the nasty saddle tramps. Jean Baptiste, who was waiting on the not-so-desirable customers, listened intently, then said, "Yes, my partner remembers." He almost said what his partner had said, *He remembered their smell*, but he decided to make it sound more agreeable. "The way they handled themselves like, *Cette um vrai hommes*, that is like real men, and one of them was, how do you say, the spit image of you."

185

The twin, smelly brother thought about that for a moment. He wasn't sure, 'cause he didn't speak no Frog, but that damned Frenchie might have just insulted him. But there were important matters at hand, so he decided to let it slip. Besides, none of his other men were even paying attention. The Frenchie got off easy this time!

"Did ya happen to notice which way they rode off?"

"*Oui, oui*," Jean Baptiste said, "they went *sud*, I mean south."

"Thanks," said the twin brother of the man who had been killed when he and his gang had attacked James Beckwourth and his four Crow wives.

The eleven men, nearly carbon copies of the other five, riding trashed-out horses, and looking and smelling the same as any man who simply refused to wash, rode south in hopes of finding their leader's twin brother.

"I told that son of a bitch, Johnny, to wait fer us at Vrain Trading Post, that's what I told 'em!" Jimmy, Johnny's older brother by ten minutes, said as he rode with the ten men he had gathered from God knows where. The plan had been simple, they would have fifteen men, and they were going to rape, pillage and steal their way all the way to California, and then they do some more raping, pillaging, and stealing when they got there. The plan was concocted one drunken night, when both Johnny and Jimmy were tired of sitting around a two-horse town, and they just wanted something to happen which wouldn't bore the shit out of them!

One of the eleven was a renegade Injun by the name of Scout, and he was doing his name by tracking the southern route out of Vrain Trading Post.

"They go here," Scout said, pointing with his arm down the road to the south.

"How ya know it's them?" Jimmy asked.

"This horse, three shoes," Scout said.

"Yeah, that's my brother's ride, a three-shoe-horse like it was a normal thing to do."

———

After two days of hearing how he'd lived the life he couldn't remember, James Pierson Beckwourth was looking over the four horses that they had brought up from the fight early that week. He saw how badly all their feet had been treated, and he simply fell into trimming, taking shoes off, and he even heated up the forge with the bellows which Uzziah had built out in the barn.

Uzziah walked out from one of the cabins and, seeing the smoke from the barn, turned to Immanuel. "Is the barn on fire?"

"No, just the forge that Beckwourth fired up."

"Why he do that?" Uzziah asked.

"I believe he's working on those mangy horses we picked up from them dead guys."

"That's great! Do you read him anything about him being a blacksmith?" Uzziah asked.

"No, ain't got that far, I don't think?"

"Well, I read ahead, and he trained as one. This is good, maybe he's remembering?"

"Well, it'll be a hell of a life for him from here on out, if he don't," Immanuel noted.

They wandered into the barn, and Beckwourth was handling a five-pound hammer like it was a toy. He had heated up a couple shoes and was pounding them into shape.

"Ya doin' that like ya know how," Uzziah asked.

"Yeah. Kinda like the hand talking. I was looking at the poor horses y'all got from that gang, and the next thing I know, I'd fired up the forge," he said as he took the shaped shoe and dunked it in the water vat. It steamed and sizzled nicely, then he worked on it cold for a bit.

"Ya really are good at this," Uzziah said, trying to compliment the man.

"Thanks, it sorta makes ya forget everything else, if ya know what I mean?" Beckwourth said as he examined the shoe and set it aside.

"I do, I do know what ya mean," Uzziah said, glad that someone else felt the same way about blacksmithing as he did.

———

Scout, the renegade Injun who was traveling with the band of saddle tramps who had concocted the bright idea of raping, pillaging and stealing their way to California, only to begin the same regime all over again, stood with a bandana wrapped around his nose and mouth. He had found something, but he wasn't too sure Jimmy was going to be happy about it.

The bloated bodies of his missing twin, Johnny, and his four compatriots lay in disarray the way they had fallen in battle around a burned-out campfire.

"What the hell happened here? I mean what the hell happened here!?" Jimmy asked the renegade scout.

"Looks like brother gunned down, and stuck by"—
he looked around—"at least seven others."

"Seven against five, now them is good odds, real fair,
huh!?" Jimmy was getting worked up into one of his
moods, and the other saddle tramps were giving him a
lot of space.

"Five Indian ponies, no shoes, two with shoes,"
Scout remarked as he studied the ground.

"Two of them Injuns had horses with shoes!?"
Jimmy asked, not understanding.

"No, five Indian ponies, two white ponies," Scout
corrected, and all the others thought this would probably be the end of Scout.

"God damn if it don't stink here!" Jimmy yelled.
"Boys, find something to do with those bloated bodies,
ya hear?"

The other nine looked between themselves, none of
them were willing to do anything.

————

About halfway between where the outlaw Jimmy was
cursing in God's name, and where James Beckwourth
was busy trimming and shoeing horses, Leah who had
once stayed with Immanuel and Uzziah, then been
taken to the place she was in to marry Oscar Blanchard's younger brother, Willet, sat snapping green
beans with the woman that she had come to admire and
love, Ophelia Blanchard.

"When did them boys say they'd be back?" Leah
asked, stretching her back out, which only made her
pregnant belly poke out even more.

"They didn't, Leah. Out chere when somebody

189

goes huntin' they come back when they come back," Ophelia said, knowing that men do the damnest things for the damnest reasons, but not wanting to get into it with her sister-in-law, Leah.

There was a crying sound from the bigger of the two cabins on the place, the settlement which Oscar and his brother, Willet, had enlarged since the marriage of Willet and Leah.

"That'd be Charlie, I think. Will don't cry that much no more," Ophelia said as she got up and walked into the bigger cabin. The crying stopped and when she walked out again, she was holding Charlie in her arms, and Will, about five years old, was holding onto her dress and sucking his thumb.

"Stop that suckin'!" Ophelia said, slapping the hand with the wet thumb away from her eldest boy's mouth.

Leah looked at Will.

"He's just misses yer teat," Leah said.

"Yeah, but he's old enough to eat nothin' but solid food, and Charlie needs the milk."

"Oscar told me yer milk tastes good!" Leah said.

"He did, did he?" Ophelia said, looking over her spectacles at Leah.

"You let him drink it, why can't his boy?" Leah did not know how to let a subject drop.

Ophelia covered Will's ears with both her hands and said, "Well, if Will could fuck me as good as my Oscar, I guess I jest might let 'im!" Ophelia said, letting go of Will's ears.

Leah's mouth was open, and she couldn't believe some of the things that came from her sister-in-law's mouth when the men were gone.

"Do you talk thataway around yer husband?" Leah asked, just hoping to send Ophelia into a snit.

"It ain't any yer business what a man and woman say to one another when they're in the throes of fucking, now is it?"

"Ya didn't cover Will's ear that time, he's a gonna start usin' that word, and Oscar's gonna know how you talk," Leah said, snapping beans faster as the conversation got nastier.

"Oh, well," Ophelia said, acting like she didn't care what Oscar knew, but she really did. She sure hoped Leah would be on her side, like she wanted all women on her side. She knew that out there in the frontier, it was man against nature and man against woman. It seemed to Ophelia that since Oscar's brother, Willet, had shown up that he was less communicative with her and spent a lot of his time talking with his brother. Well, they were brothers, suppose she shouldn't have understood that, but it literally irritated the shite out of her.

"Are ya okay?" Leah asked.

"I am, and I do hope we can continue to be the best of sister-in-laws," Ophelia said, and that, as far as Leah was concerned, came out of nowhere.

———

A huge bonfire was raging, and the last of the five bodies was thrown on it as Jimmy stood there with a scowl on his face. He hadn't thought about burying his younger brother before he, himself, died, and he sure as hell hadn't thought about having to throw his stabbed, shot, smelly, and bloated body on a bonfire, but life does put a fly in your ointment sometimes, it truly does.

"Was that Johnny?" he asked the bandana-faced men who had tossed the body in the fire.

"We don't know," one of them said.

"Whatcha mean ya don't know, either it was him, or it weren't!?"

"They been dead so long, they don't look the same," the same one answered.

"I am gonna get them sons a bitches that did this to my twin brother. Ya know we twins, we got a special connection, I knew somethin' was up, I knew he was in trouble, and ifn he'd only waited on me, well, this wouldn't have happened!"

The wind changed directions, and the stench of the five burning bodies blew back on the gang of bad hombres. They all complained and moved to the other side of the raging bonfire.

"I find trail," it was Scout.

"Which way does it lead?"

He pointed in a westerly direction.

"Mount up, boys, we're burnin' daylight!" Jimmy said as they rode off with Scout leading the way.

4

Oscar and his brother, Willet, had enjoyed their childhood together. They had dreamed that someday they would be like the men that their father had read to them about in the newspaper. Little did Mr. Blanchard know that his tales, some of them tall, about the men who were winning the west would stick right in the hearts of his two sons. They played games that centered around Indians and the west. Their father had built them a treehouse out back in a sycamore tree, and sometimes the floor of that treehouse would be the pilot house in a paddle steamer, and sometimes, a canoe as they made their way up the Mighty Mo the way Lewis and Clarke had done. Little do they, or any of us, for that matter, know that childhood dreams were a bit more than they seemed. They were, in fact, a grand architect's plans for what we could become if we followed those dreams.

Oscar had been the first to leave, and when he'd sent for his brother, Willet, and Willet had quit his good job at the mercantile store there in town, everybody knew that it would come to no good end. But here the two brothers were engaged in a battle with nature, the natives who lived within that nature, and of course, the evil which exists everywhere.

"Did ya ever think we'd be together out here like this?" Oscar asked Willet.

"No, I still have to pinch myself to make sure it's not a dream. I wish I had been there when ya saved Uzziah and Immanuel's life," Willet mused.

"Look, brother, there will be plenty of chances out here to test our metal against the west and the rest of the world."

"I know, but at the wedding, when I heard Immanuel talking about how ya'd just drilled the guy who had planned to do them in, I don't know. The look in Immanuel and Uzziah's eyes when they looked at you. Yer a hero to them, ya know that, don't ya?"

Oscar drew his horse up close to his brother Willet. "Willet, we're all heroes out here, and the important thing to remember is ya got a good wife in Leah—"

"That I do, she's a marvel under the sheets," Willet said, looking wistful.

"Ya don't have to tell me, why do ya think we built the other smaller cabin? All yer rutting was keeping Ophelia and I up at night!"

"Oh, I am sorry, brother, truly I am!"

"Hey, don't look now, but over on the next crest is a very nice-looking deer, be a hero now!"

Willet did not dismount, he had trained the horse to accept firing going off his back. He sighted in as best he could, then fired!

———

Oscar and his little brother Willet had made it back to the settlement right before sunset. They had them a long drink from the fine well they had dug, and the women went out into the barn and began cutting up the one deer which they had managed to bring down.

"They's out there, actin' like they done killed a herd of buffs," Leah said, taking the boning knife and cutting down the length of the carcass.

"Well, they's men, and their quests, or hunts or whatever ya wanna call them, they take serious-like," Ophelia said, trying to justify the fact that she and Leah were now doing all the work, when they had been doing nothing but work since the men left.

"Yeah, but they didn't walk out to get the meat, they rode, and then a couple shots, and they rode back with it." Leah was not feeling well, and she knew that it was possible the baby might be on the way any minute.

"How's yer back?" Ophelia asked, trying to change the subject.

"Awful, just awful, was it that way when you was in the family way?"

"Everybody's got it different, all I know is, soon as it's here, ya won't mind what ya went through."

They heard a fluttering at the tumbler's coop, and Leah stopped cutting.

"I'll go check," she said and went out the back man door, and taking the tumbler who hadn't quite settled in yet, took the small message from the container on its leg.

She walked back into the barn, unraveling the note.

"Who's it from?"

"Like we got more than one set of mens that we communicates with?" she asked, reading the note.

"Well, what's it say?"

"It's nothing," Leah said, setting the piece of rolled-up paper on the milking stool. Ophelia came over, unrolled it, and read.

"Aw, that's nice, just checking in, they are," she said.

"Yeah, sitting up on that mountain top of theirs with their four cabins and nothing to do, I swear the next time I'm born I'm comin' back a man!"

Ophelia laughed and laughed, and that got Leah to laughing.

"Don't, it hurts my tummy," she said, which made Ophelia laugh more, and Leah joined in.

"What y'all laughing at?" Oscar asked, then noticing the hanging dead deer, said, "My God, ladies, what ya been doing back chere?!" Then he yelled to Willet, "Come on in chere, boy, or we ain't gonna have any supper 'til spring!"

The ladies were glad to be rid of the cutting up of the deer as Willet and Oscar took over in their manly way. Ophelia was glad to be rid of the work, and they pretended to be proud of their men, who knew how to do what they had already been doing.

Scout had the trail all right, and he was following it with great intent, but when he went up on the rise to see what lay ahead, he couldn't help but notice the smoke in the distance. It was steady and a straight line to heaven. It was off the course of the men they were chasing, but the way those five had met their deaths, Scout wasn't too sure he wanted to catch up with the hombres who had done that. He decided, since he was the one tracking, that it would be more interesting to see what was going on where the smoke was rising, so that's what he did.

As he turned away from the trail of those who had done in Jimmy's brother, he smiled to himself, when everyone else, too worried about what they were chattering about, all nonsense, they didn't even notice he'd changed directions, howsoever slightly.

———

Uzziah and Immanuel were standing, leaning against the railing in the barn. They had just watched James Beckwourth trim and shoe every horse in the place, even theirs. He was a natural.

"Where'd ya learn to do that?" Immanuel asked.

"Don't know,' Beckwourth said, wiping his hands clean.

"Well, I do," Immanuel started in. "This is the trade ya learned after yer pa set ya free, it's right there in the journals."

"That so?"

"Yeah, it means ya probably are rememberin' things, right, Immanuel," Uzziah asked his partner.

"It don't mean any such thing," Beckwourth said, sort of disgusted. "All it proves is that I got memory in my body, but not in my noggin."

"Maybe, maybe not. Your wives are fixing those rabbits we shot this afternoon, come and listen to more of yer stories," Uzziah offered.

"They ain't my wives, no matter what ya say is gonna convince me of that. Ya think I knowed their language, well, I don't, just sounds like gibberish to me."

Immanuel looked at Uzziah as Beckwourth walked

back to the cabin he'd been staying in. At least they didn't have to worry about him running off again.

"What ya thinkin'?" Uzziah asked.

"That it might take the rest of his life to remember the first part of it."

"Yeah, does seem that way, don't it? Hell of a thing, ain't it?"

"Yeah. We need somethin' shocking, something which will pull him out of himself, and let the real man, old bloody arm, step forward," Immanuel said.

"Is that what they called him, bloody arm?"

"Yeah, that should tell ya something."

"Well, let me know when ya find out what the magic bullet is that will help him on his journey back to hisself," Uzziah said, putting the forge to bed.

———

They were getting so close to that fire that Scout had smelled the venison long before any of the White men. Finally, Jimmy spoke up.

"Hey, somebody's cooking deer meat!"

Thank the Great Spirit, thought Scout, *now, maybe they have some fun.*

Not three miles away, Leah and Ophelia were finishing up the supper dishes as the men, Oscar and Willet, sat on the porch, in rockers they'd made, and were smoking their pipes.

"Do ya smoke?" Leah asked Ophelia.

"Heavens no, it's a nasty habit! Why?"

"Ifn we smoked, they could be doing the dishes and we'd be relaxing."

"You need that baby to come, that's all that's wrong with ya," Ophelia said.

The rank gang had spotted the cabins and the barn, and they saw within the warming lights inside a life that they would never have. And like all men who cannot create life, they reveled in destroying it. Jimmy had his binocs out and was spying on their latest victims.

"There's two womens in the cabin closest to us, and two men, that's all I see, and they're nowhere to be seen," Jimmy said, snickering.

"Well, let's go dip our wicks, huh?" one of the boys suggested.

Jimmy grabbed the one who had spoken and pushed him up against a tree.

"We will do as I say, just like always, ifn ya can't wait, then go off there and choke yer chicken for all I care," Jimmy said, and that got snickers from his crew.

Will, five years old and very curious, was standing on a chair in the back bedroom of Oscar and Ophelia's cabin. He loved the wildlife that surrounded the cabins and could sit for hours watching it. There was a pond back away from the cabins where a stream ran into it, then came back out the other side. Will loved to watch the game that came to water every night, and was puzzled when his pa and the other man had to ride distances to get game. He had said as much to his father, but was told that game was special and if they started shooting it now, then when winter came there'd be nothing near the cabins to shoot.

As Will was watching, he looked over and Charles had fallen asleep with a bottle of milk in his hands. That milk had been taken from his mother's teats, and even though they said he was too old for that milk, well, it didn't stop him from loving it. He got down and very gingerly took the bottle, climbed back up in the window and started sucking. *Now, this is the life*, Will thought. But as he watched so contented with his mother's milk flowing into his tummy, he noticed some shiny things which were reflecting off something out by the pond. The animals who came every night to drink had scurried off, and Will knew that could only mean that men were out there at the pond. Then, with the reflection of the moon off the pond, he saw the shapes of many men and many horses as they came silently toward his home.

Will was smart enough not to go tell his pa. He had been told the story about when his pa had gone off and left his mama and him, and some men came and did bad things to his mama, and almost got him killed, too. She would react instead of putting him off.

"Mama, mama," he said in his scared little boy's voice, which had Ophelia running to him, and listening, "Hosses, mens!" he said and pointed toward the pond.

———

Jimmy was sure these people were going to get one hell of a surprise. Well, there would be a surprise, but it might not be the folks in the house.

———

As soon as Will had alerted his mama, she sent Leah to the barn to send a message to Uzziah and Immanuel, then she rallied the men, who took their big knives and snuck into the woods out back, going around the long way to the pond.

The last of Jimmy's men had tied their horses to trees and were sneaking up behind the majority of the group when they were seized from behind and their throats cut. As they tried to scream, the air went out the cut and didn't cross their windpipe.

As the silent march toward the destruction of the family in the cabins continued, two more men were knifed in the throat, and the lights from the cabin were making it impossible for them to get any more kills. Oscar and Willet ran around to the barn and scared Leah as she released the tumbler into the air.

"Stop playin' with the pigeons, girl, and get into the house," Willet scolded her. She looked at him to say something smart back, but when she saw the blood all over his arms, she ran to the house ahead of the two men.

Oscar had built a saferoom of sorts after the last time that man had raped Ophelia and almost killed the baby. It was a root cellar, supposedly, but really it was a big enough root cellar to fit everybody and then some. And Willet had tunneled from the root cellar to his cabin, and therefore both places could enjoy the safety of that retreat.

———

As the men got closer, Jimmy whispered to Scout, "Where's those other boys?"

The Injun shrugged and all Jimmy could think about was the fact that his seconds on the quim would happen a lot sooner if those four bastards had decided to sit this one out.

———

The two families didn't go directly into the root cellar. They sent the women and the two children down there, and since it was the place of last resort, and from what Willet and Oscar had counted, there were only seven left, it might not be that bad.

There was a knock at the door, which was answered by a double ought buckshot which tore through that door, and had Scout scrambling away.

That's when everybody there just started shooting at the cabin where everybody seemed to be.

Holes were being torn in the cabin, and Willet and Oscar hit the floor and prayed no one would be shooting low. Lamps were hit, and splashed their oil on the floor, and that ignited into flames. Willet was at the fire with one of the rugs by the fireplace, and he beat out the flames as shots ricocheted around him. He was hit in the leg, just a scratch, but it hurt like hell. Oscar answered that by standing and emptying his Winchester out the window, which got all Jimmy's men running for cover.

"We need food and water for our horses," came Jimmy's voice.

Oscar and Willet just looked at each other. Finally Oscar shouted, "Well, come on in and get it!"

———

"He's being a smartass, ain't he?" Jimmy said to Scout.

"What's a smartass?" Scout asked and Jimmy threw his hand away in a gesture which just meant, *What does an Injun know?*

"Okay, okay, so we don't want that, we wants yer women, send them out and we'll let the rest of ya live," Jimmy said, never knowing just how cowardly men could be.

———

Ophelia heard all this and couldn't help but think of Lot's daughter. In chapter 19 of the book of Genesis, Lot shows hospitality to two angels who arrive in Sodom, and invites them to stay in his home. But the men of Sodom, who were against hospitality in the first place, asked Lot to send his two guests out so that they can literally sodomize them. Lot admonished the Sodomites for their wickedness, then offers them his two virgin daughters, but when they refuse, wanting the men instead, the angels strike them blind and warns Lot and his family to get out of the city of Sodom.

Why, she wondered to herself, *would I remember such a thing in this horrible situation?*

"Come on in, the quim is fine," Willet said, then turned to his brother. "I hope Leah didn't hear that, I'll catch hell!" and the two men chuckled.

Leah turned to Ophelia and whispered, "Does he think I'm deaf as well as pregnant!?!"

"Bring out the womens, or we'll burn the place down," Jimmy said.

———

Uzziah was cleaning out the pigeon coop, and it was one nasty job. He was thinking that that was where the expression came from, *Dirty Birds*. And the next time someone called him a *dirty bird*, there were going to be fighting words.

He heard a tumbler overhead and looked up. Sure enough, there one was circling like she wanted to come land. She tumbled a few times, like she was wounded, but Uzziah knew that was just their way of getting away from predator birds. He was in the way, he knew that, but he was almost finished, and the birds already in the coop seemed to appreciate the job he was doing.

"Hey, there's a tumbler tryin' to land, yer in the way," Immanuel yelled at him.

"Ya don't think I knows that, fer Crickey's sake," Uzziah yelled back.

"What's all the shouting about?" It was James Beckwourth, who didn't know he was James Beckwourth, but he did seem to be getting better with each day. Who knew? Maybe some day it would all come back to him, in the meantime, he was the two mountain men's guest, and so were his four wives. *It was taking a powerful lot of hunting to keep a crew of seven fed*, Immanuel thought.

"Oh, just one of our tumblers trying to roost. Uzziah sent a message to some friends of ours down in the foothills, it's probably their answer."

"You can send messages by pigeons?" James asked.

"Sure can. Uzziah, move away from the coop unless ya want me to beat ya round the head and shoulders!" Immanuel screamed.

"Ya just try it, ya no good scummy bastard, ya smell

like my feet and they ain't been washed in a coon's age," Uzziah yelled back.

"I thought you two were friends," Beckwourth said.

"We is, but—hey, hafta apologize for Uzziah's coon comment," Immanuel said.

"Well, you's a coon, ain't ya?" Uzziah asked.

"And a nigger and a mulato, so coon is okay with me, just don't go all squaw on me," Beckwourth said to Immanuel.

"I promise I won't—Uzziah!" Immanuel shouted at his partner.

Uzziah, giving Immanuel a really dirty look—one of his best, Immanuel would have to admit—moved away from the coop, and then the bird overhead, tumbled a couple more times, then came to the roost.

"And I'm gettin' the message," Immanuel said as he headed for the coop.

"No, ya ain't, I cleaned the coop and it's my message, I sent one to the families and now, this one's mine," Uzziah said, reaching into the coop, right as Immanuel grabbed Uzziah's leg and pulled him to the ground.

"I said, it's mine, and that's what I meant!" Immanuel started to go for the bird who had just flown in, the one carrying the message, and Uzziah kicked his legs out from under him. Immanuel grabbed Uzziah's leg and brought him down on the ground with him, and the two men rolled around in the pine needles, slugging at each other and swearing oaths.

James Beckwourth and his four Crow wives stood there like a dutiful audience, and laughed as the two men had at each other but were really doing no harm.

Beckwourth saw the little tube on the bird's leg, the

one who had just come to roost. The other tumblers had them too, but he surmised that the new arrival had a message in the little tube. He reached right in, and being gentle as all get out, got the message and let the bird go back into the coop.

Uzziah and Immanuel looked up at Beckwourth and both yelled, "That was my message!"

James read, "Come now, varmints attacking! Leah."

"Hey, ya can read again!" Immanuel said, so glad that he would not have to strain his eyes and read from those journals.

"Yeah, guess I can," Beckwourth said, smiling.

Uzziah took the message from the Black man's hand. "Y'all forgettin' the message, they's in trouble! Let's ride!"

There was a short argument whether Beckwourth and his four Crow wives should go, but in the manner of an emergency, Beckwourth won simply because they didn't have time to object long enough.

Within fifteen minutes, they were all gunned up, well, the Crow wives took bow and arrows from what the two mountain men could only surmise was a war bag. The seven of them were riding down the mountain, and with all intents and purposes, to rescue those folks in the foothills. It would take them two days of easy riding, but Uzziah figured if they rode hard and rested the horses, it would be just over a day. It was sunset now, so they'd probably arrive at the settlement just after sundown tomorrow.

5

Back at the settlement, their last thoughts would have been on any kind of rescue from anybody. Willet had been wounded in the arm, and Ophelia had bandaged that up nicely. Just as she was about through bandaging Willet and getting his arm in a sling, the men out there threw a homemade torch onto the roof of Oscar and Ophelia's cabin. They had shake singles, not being able to afford anything else, not that anything else was available in the foothills of the Rockies when they built their cabin.

One of the bad hombres had another torch and was running toward the house when Oscar shot him in the leg. He went down, but not before throwing the second torch, which fell short of the house.

"I got 'im!" Oscar yelled in triumph.

"Good man!" his younger brother Willet encouraged him.

"He's hobblin' back," Oscar yelled, and Willet, one armed, laid his rifle in the gun cut in the shutter, and fired.

The man screamed out, both his arms shooting up like he was praising Jesus, whom it looked like he was about to see, and he fell dead!

"Ya killed him and you with a busted-up arm!" Oscar congratulated his brother. Later, they might just admit that living out the dream they had when they were kids was a bit more involved than the dream had let on.

"That's one less asshole to worry about!" Willet yelled.

"Willet, the children, please think about yer words!" Leah yelled at him.

"Sorry, honey, I really am," he said as the larger of the two cabins, the one they were in, began to fill with smoke.

"Ma, done heard worse from Pa," the five-year-old Will remarked.

"Son, now's not the time," Oscar scolded.

"But when them out there is dead, it most certainly will be the time!" Ophelia scolded her husband.

"Grab everything ya can carry thatcha wanna keep, we're goin' next door," Oscar said.

"But they'll just burn our place down, too, Oscar!" Leah complained.

"We gotcha the tin roof outta St. Louis, Leah, don't ya remember?"

"That's right, twas expensive, but about to pay fer itself!" Willet said as he was grabbing things his wife Leah was handing him. "You okay, honey?" he asked her because she was holding her tummy.

"I'm pregnant with yer child, Willet, and thems out there is tryin' to kill us all, no, I am not okay!?!"

Willet rolled his eyes as Oscar opened the trapdoor, revealing the stairs that went down into the root cellar. The cabin was roiling with smoke by the time they all got down there. Hams were hanging from the root cellar ceiling, which was the big cabin's floor, and Oscar grabbed a couple of them on his way to the secret passage.

Over against the wall which was closest to Willet and Leah's cabin, there was a bunch of shelves which had canned stuff on them. He toppled the shelf, and the glass jars hit the dirt floor and smashed.

"Damn it, Oscar, ya ruint my matters!" Ophelia yelled at him.

"Mama's swearing now, Pa," Will noted, and he got a crop on the ear for that. He didn't yell out, just looked at his ma like he wanted to do something.

"There's two sets of rules, son," Oscar said. "One fer us, and one fer them."

"Shut up, both of ya!" Ophelia yelled.

"There ain't no time for arguing," Willet said. "Where's the tunnel door?"

Oscar yanked a tarp down, and behind it, there was the four-foot-high tunnel, they would all have to bend low to get through. Sparks and soot were falling through the spaces between the floorboards upstairs, and they hustled to get through to the other side. Oscar had been smart and put sticks of dynamite at the entrance to the tunnel when they were all through, he ran back and lit the fuse sticking out from the ceiling of the tunnel, running back real fast, he slammed the door that led into Willet's root cellar.

"Get down everybody!" he yelled as he threw himself to the floor of Willet's root cellar.

———

Outside and their faces glowing in the cabin fire which they had started, the remaining six bad hombres, headed up by Jimmy, stood at the edge of the woods which faced the cabin.

"Remember when they's come runnin' out, don't shoot the womens!" Jimmy yelled at them.

"If carry rifle, shoot!" the Renegade said.

"No, even if they're carrin' a rifle, do not shoot the quim! Ya stupid renegade, that jest cost ye yer first turn at the pussy!"

"Get ready!" someone yelled, and all rifles and pistols were pointed at the cabin's front door. The line of men with guns walked closer and closer as no one emerged.

The cabin exploded high into the air, carrying boards, square horseshoe nails, and sundries high into the night. The explosion also went outward, throwing flames and the same sort of detritus at the men who had crept closer and closer from the edge of the woods.

Jimmy and his men were thrown back well into the woods where they incurred many an injury, but unfortunately, no one was killed.

"What in the name of Christ!" Billy shouted as he picked himself up and checked for injuries to his person. "That went off like a powder keg was inside!"

"Kill killers in dying death," Scout said, proud of the people they had been trying to get at, that they had decided to go out literally with a bang. As far as Scout was concerned, these people had good medicine and were brave.

Twenty minutes later, the fire had died down on

the big cabin, and Jimmy and his men were standing there with their mouths open.

"They die fire, much brave, good deaths," Scout said, and was rewarded by the butt of Jimmy's rifle hitting him in the face. He went back and got up fast with his knife drawn. Jimmy's rifle cocked and pointed right at Scout.

"Break teeth!" Scout said, spitting out pieces of his teeth.

"Break heart," Jimmy said, placing the end of the barrel on Scout's chest. "You'll be a dead redskin and we'll be humpin' away without ya!"

"No hump ashes," Scout said, his voice slightly changed from the damage done to his mouth.

"They died like that, and I was the one who threw the first torch," a wrangler said.

"Boo-who!" Jimmy said. "We didn't know they's crazy now did we? Let's go see what we can scavenge from the other cabin," he said, and before he could take a step, the sorrow-filled wrangler who had thrown the first torch, ran for the front door of the other cabin.

"Wait, ya fool!" Jimmy warned.

"Finders keepers, losers weepers!" the wrangler yelled over his shoulder, as a shotgun blast tore through him and he went down like a rag doll.

The remaining five men jumped behind whatever cover they could find as rifles, shotguns, and pistols were peppering the woods.

Lying on his back, Jimmy spoke up between his teeth, "They had a tunnel, a damned tunnel!"

By the end of the first day, both Uzziah and Immanuel were amazed at the fortitude of James Beckwourth and his four Crow wives. When they stopped to rest a bit, the five of them remained on their horse while the horses drank from a stream, and as soon as both the mountain men were mounted James and the four squaws were first to head out.

"I'm plumb tuckered out!" Uzziah yelled over at Immanuel, the two of them the last to leave the last rest stop.

"They ain't!" Immanuel said and let it be at that.

"Well, there's a kind road real soon, and we won't have to be dodgin' rocks and such," Uzziah grunted.

"That's good, what ya figure, how much more time, afore we get there?" Immanuel asked.

"It'll probably be false dawn by then," Uzziah said and got back to hunkering down in the saddle.

———

Jimmy didn't know what to do. They were running low on ammo, and they hadn't exactly planned to stay anyplace for this long. What little food they did have, they'd cooked, and the whiskey was gone, and boy oh boy, this idea was beginning to stink to high heaven.

"Boss?"

"Yeah, Mumford, what is it?"

"We should just go while the goin's good."

Jimmy actually thought about that, they had started out on the trail of the men who had killed his twin brother Johnny and now they were hungry, almost out of bullets, and the quim that they so desired had cost them

—what? Six of them were dead, four as they snuck up, that was a joke, they must have seen them coming. Some eagle-eyed frontiersman must have been at the window when they were sneaking by the pond. Little did he know that a five-year-old boy can be eagle-eyed! This was circling down into a thing which had no beginning and no end. It was downright depressing! But his ma used to always say, *It's always darkest afore the dawn!*

Besides, he could taste that quim, he could, and he was going to have some, even if it cost him everything he had.

"Nah, we ain't gonna cut and run," Jimmy said.

"Why not?"

"We'd never live it down being bettered by a bunch of sodbusters."

"That's true," Mumford said, then added, "But who'd hafta know?"

It was a question to consider, but even the smartest outlaw tells tales out of school, and this bunch was not even close to being the dumbest of the smartest! Down the road, he'd hear about it, how some damned farmers up in the foothills had killed half his gang and nearly blown them to kingdom come. No, he was going to win this, he was!

"That ain't the point, Mumford."

"It ain't?"

"No, I'd know, and don't know if I could live with meself after a bunch of pussy farmers chased us off!"

"Sure, wouldn't want that gettin' round," Mumford agreed sort of sarcastically.

"Let's pepper the cabin with all we got!" Jimmy said, and they opened up.

———

Inside, those who were dodging bullets had no idea that this was the bad hombres' last hurrah, for all they knew, they had a thousand more rounds apiece.

Leah was covered as best she could be by Willet, who took a slug through his side. Oscar laid behind a table with Ophelia, spooning up right beside him, and then Will was spooning, and finally, Charlie spooned up against five-year-old Will.

———

It felt like the firing went on forever when it probably only lasted eight or so minutes. They were plumb out of shells and about to just go when a voice spoke up from the cabin.

———

Before Ophelia spoke, the situation in the cabin was assessed.

Willet was bleeding badly from a through-and-through in his right side. And Oscar, Oscar had two slugs that were still in his back, but his spooning had worked. The slugs had gone through the solid oak table, then into him, but they hadn't totally penetrated him, and his wife Ophelia was safe, and so were their children.

Leah hadn't been hit, but it looked like she was getting ready to have the baby, so what was Ophelia to do? The only able-bodied person, that's what she was, and she had to make a decision that might save them all, or maybe it wouldn't.

"Oscar, can ya hear me?"

"Yeah, a'course," he said with pain in his voice.

"I'm gonna go out there and stall those bastards," Ophelia said.

"What!?" Oscar asked, not believing what he was hearing.

"No, Ophelia, ya can't," it was Leah, and her face looked like a birthing mother's face.

"I can, and I am," she said.

"Why!?!" Oscar asked.

"'Cause ifn I play it right, I can keep the others from comin' in here and cuttin' Leah's baby from her belly so that they can fuck her, and me, too, and you two boys, they will just outright kill!"

Will looked from his mama to his pa, and he didn't know what to make of anything now.

Leah heard what her friend had said, and it wasn't like she hadn't thought about it, she had, and she knew somewhere in what her friend had said was a terrible truth. Even if she lived, could she witness the baby which she and Willet had made, cut from her, his brains smashed against the fireplace hearth? Could she do that?"

"Ophelia's right," Leah whispered.

Both the wounded men looked at her, and so did Will, Ophelia's son.

"Mama, don't go to the bad men," he said, crying.

"It's the only way to buy us some time. Leah, ya sent that tumbler to Uzziah, did ya not?"

"I did."

"Good girl, thought that's what ya was doin' out

there before ya ran in. There's whiskey in the root cellar, right, Willet?"

"Yes, ma'am," he said, already ashamed of what he was about to let happen.

"Once I leave, ya bar and bolt the door, do the same to the winders, they can't burn ya out, ya got a tin roof, and ifn anybody gets close enough to burn the sides, kill 'em through the shutter cuts, okay?" Ophelia said looking around at her family, at Oscar, the man she loved, and had built this living with, the man who had somehow managed not exactly to forget about what the man was doing when he killed him, and maybe, just maybe he could forgive, she didn't expect him to forget, but forgive again, maybe, if she lived, wouldn't he? Little Will ran to her, and she held him. Charlie was right behind him.

"Kill 'em, Mama," Charlie said just like the half-breed he was.

Ophelia went to the root cellar, got the bottles of whiskey, and changed into Leah's best dress. It was tight, but that was good, it pushed her teats out so she looked seductive.

At the front door, she stopped. "I love all y'all," she said, and was out the door. They could hear her yelling to the men as they bolted and locked the door.

———

They had gathered their horses, well, the ones that hadn't been killed by the sodbusters, and were about to mount up and leave when a woman's voice cut through the air.

"Who wants some whiskey and pussy?" Ophelia shouted out.

Jimmy had his left foot in the stirrup and was about to swing up, and sure enough, that stopped him. He got down and spoke to the remaining members of the gang.

"This might be another damn sodbuster trick so play it cool, I'll check it out."

When he got to the clearing where the cabins had been built, the smoke was still rising toward the full moon, and in front of the other cabin and walking his way was an attractive woman dressed like a soiled dove, her enormous breast spilling from her tight dress, and in her hands, two bottles of what looked like bonded whiskey.

"Do you have any idea how long it's been since I seen bonded whiskey?" Jimmy asked.

"Well, let's build up a fire, and I'll take down my drawers and boy, I am hot fer you fellas," Ophelia said as she swiped one of the bottles and caught up her dress, and pulled it up far enough for Jimmy to see, that, in fact, she had on no drawers at all!

"Yer naked underneath that purty dress," Jimmy said.

"As a jaybird," she said, walking right by him and toward the other men.

———

In the cabin, all they could hear was the sound of someone playing a guitar, and all the men laughing, and behind, or was it rising above their laughter, there was the sound of Ophelia's laugh. It was a bit strained and unnatural, but those men wouldn't know that. She was shouting and cavorting, then everything went quiet except for the music as the quim party started. Oscar fought down his revulsion for the woman he loved. She was and probably had been all along, their only hope. She had laid down, not quite her life, but she had laid down, and the murderous men were plunging into her, shooting into her instead of shooting at them. And Ophelia was making sounds that Oscar had never heard her make. She was shouting for them to get harder, and plunge deeper, and her voice sounded drunk, and it probably was.

———

A line had formed, which led to a buckboard that someone had scavenged from the barn. They broke the front wheels down and it was at just the right level for the woman to lie on. She had taken all her clothes off, and to tell the truth, for some of those men, it was the first time they had seen a fully naked woman that wasn't painted in a picture on a saloon wall. She had her legs spread and up with her knees bent, and a bottle in one hand and the next man's dick in the other, getting him ready when the one who was humping her was through.

Ophelia was drunker that she ever imagined she could be, and as the men went through the line once, then having more whiskey, started through again, she tried to remember that this wasn't rape, if she didn't resist, and her hole was sore, but what was that compared to her babies' deaths and her husband's mutilation?

"Come on! Come on!" she coaxed the next man,

and he was young, and his staff was fully erected as he drove into her time and time again.

"Give it all to me!" she screamed, knowing that her voice was shredding Oscar's heart, and that if she lived, he would never, ever forgive her. "Fuck me good!" she screamed and that acclamation was joined by men's shouts and laughing. Truth be told, these men had never had a woman like Ophelia, they had no idea that her passion was born from love, not for them, not from what they were standing in line to do to her, but for her family.

As it was Jimmy's third time, and he was ready, oh boy what a whore this one was, she must have been a soiled dove before the sodbuster convinced her to marry him. And now, her wildest dreams were coming true as she got to fuck through the night, and five men, just enough for everyone to be ready when his time came. Some of the men were so horny, they got up on the buckboard, and jerked off on her, their cum shooting out and hitting her on the face, that was the idea, that was the target, and when they scored, they shouted with glee with the other men encouraging them.

"She's a mess, clean yerself up, whore," Jimmy asked none too nicely.

She walked down to the stream, well, she waddled as her hips felt like they had been displaced by the continual thrusting of the men into her. She washed in the stream, scooping handfuls of water and throwing them against her nearly ruptured vagina. When she walked from the stream, the Injun, who had been the gentlest with her, stopped her.

"Bear grease," was all he said, and she nodded, and taking the bear grease, rubbed it all up inside her, and

219

along her legs, which were chaffed. It felt much better, and now the men would slide without her having to supply the slide.

———

Inside the cabin, safe from what was going on out there, Oscar, with his two back wounds, gathered up a gun and headed for the door.

"Oscar, what are ya doin'?" It was Willet, whose side wound had stopped bleeding.

"I can't stand it. I'm gonna go out there and put Ophelia out of her misery!" he said as he tried to undo the barred door, but didn't have the strength.

"She's enjoying it, Oscar, can't ya hear her encouraging them, she likes it!" Willet whispered into his brother's ear.

Oscar looked at Willet, his brother, and broke down into tears. Willet held him up well enough, 'til Leah came over and helped Willet carry his brother Oscar to their blood-soaked bed, where he collapsed and burst into tears.

———

Back at the broken-down wagon, the buckboard, she laid down and Jimmy felt his cock slide easily into her, and it felt good, and her tits were jiggling nicely, and he was so hot for her.

"Kiss me," she whispered to him, and when he bent over her to kiss her, all he could smell was the cum of other men, but he forced himself to her mouth, and as he laid his lips on her she bit him through his bottom lip.

"You bitch!" he screamed and he clobbered her a couple times, and she was out, probably exactly what she had wanted him to do. He looked at the others, who looked like they'd been told there was no Santa Claus, and he noticed it was false dawn already. They had fucked this sodbuster's wife for most of the night.

6

The evening had turned coolish, and Uzziah knew that this was the touch of autumn that usually came to this region. The night was ending now because there was grayish-like light in the east, where false dawn was announcing itself. This was the time of day, didn't matter what season, that Uzziah liked best. There was a sense of God walking in the garden when the day was this young. He looked around, knowing that the Father was all around him wherever he went, in fact, since he was a believing Christian, the Holy Spirit lived within him. His massive, overfed body was the temple of the Living God, and he relished that fact. He'd talked with Immanuel about this very fact, and although the man was elusive, Uzziah felt that his mountain man partner believed much the same. They just thought about it in different terms.

He was glad his mother Rahab had read to him from the Holy Book when he was young, and that he had grown up in a family where God was respected as the author, sustainer, and redeemer of the universe. It did a man good to walk with God, when certain things presented themselves, and unbeknownst to Uzziah, he was about to be presented with one of those things.

They were near the cabins and had been walking their horses for a while now. Beckwourth tied his horse to a tree, followed by his four wives, whom he didn't know from Adam, and Immanuel and Uzziah followed suit.

Beckwourth put his index finger to his lips, indicating that silence would be good from now on. He was able to walk through the undergrowth and sticks lying about like no one either Immanuel or Uzziah had ever seen. They tried hard to walk in his footsteps, just as his Crow wives did. It worked, the six of them walked right to the edge of whatever was happening, and it sure looked like something unholy.

Ophelia Blanchard was naked as—yes, a jaybird and lying on a buckboard which had had the back wheels broken so she was more presentable to the men who were in line.

They took the scene in and Uzziah felt bad for the Crow women, but evidently, they had seen, or been a part of, a scene like this before. Other than their upper lips sneering, they certainly didn't look away. Then came the big surprise.

"What's the matter? Can't ya get it up anymore?" Ophelia's voice sounded hardened and whorish as she berated the man who had kneeled before her.

"Ifn yer limp, get to the back of the line," the man behind him said. "I got a boner the size of Texas," he said, and sure enough, he did.

"Maybe I'll just piss on her instead," the man with the limp dick said.

"Not while I'm pokin' her ya won't," exclaimed the man who had just inserted his rather large cock into Ophelia and she moaned and rotated her hips so he could get the most pleasure.

It would turn out to be the damnest thing either Immanuel or Uzziah had ever seen and probably ever would see. James Pierson Beckwourth walked right into the light of the campfire and stood there a good thirty seconds before he spoke.

"Whatcha doin' fellas?" he asked rather politely, considering it must have been obvious what they were up to.

The men standing around all had their pants off, and if they had an erection before Beckwourth spoke, they certainly didn't afterward. The man closest to him went for his pants, and Beckwourth nearly cut his head off with the big knife he was carrying. That took a little time as he sawed through the man's spine.

By then, others had reached their pants and were drawing what they had forgotten were mostly emptied guns.

At the first click, click of an empty chamber, Beckwourth turned to the man who was firing an empty gun at him, and threw the knife at him, hitting him in the mouth, and the blade stuck out the back of his throat. He fell dead on the spot.

With his blood-covered arm, Beckwourth drew his piece, and it was then that Immanuel remembered why he—Beckwourth—was called *bloody arm* almost his entire fighting career.

The next man fired what little ammo he had, about

three shots, and all of them went wide of Beckwourth, who simply signaled the Crow women to get involved. The man looked like a pin cushion within seconds as arrow after arrow sank into his chest. He was looking down at them all in amazement when one entered his eye and came out the back of his head.

The others started to scatter, meaning the one man who was still standing around without his pants on skedaddled out of there.

It was then that Immanuel and Uzziah realized Ophelia was missing from the buckboard. Someone had absconded with her.

They came into the scene about that time, not having done a thing toward rescuing their friends other than watch James Beckwourth in action, and what action it was!

"Where's the woman?" Beckwourth asked, and both Uzziah and Immanuel shrugged as a horse lit out of the back of their camp. The horse was seated by Jimmy, the twin they hadn't earlier had the pleasure of killing, and behind his horse, Jimmy's hand holding the horse's reins was a naked woman, tied hand to feet, slung across another horse.

Everyone drew on the two horses, but the way he was headed, Ophelia's horse was behind him, blocking any shot. Shooting at him meant shooting at her. Everyone put their guns away.

"Let's go get 'em!" Immanuel said, but Beckwourth put out an arm and grabbed Immanuel by the collar, the one and only time Uzziah had ever seen such a thing done to the man.

"Later, we will go and get him, but first we check on the cabin not burned to the ground," Beckwourth said, and it was the way he said it that led both Immanuel and Uzziah to comply. Later that winter they would talk about that.

All seven of them walked cautiously toward the other shot-up but not burned cabin. Somebody inside must have been watching what had happened out there because a voice came from that cabin, and it was the voice of a child.

"Come quick! My pa's bleeding out!" little Will screamed.

They rushed into the cabin, and in one corner, a woman—Beckwourth would find out later her name was Leah—was in labor, with a wounded man standing nearby. The Crow women went immediately to her aid and crowded out the wounded man. He stumbled away and sat down in a chair. In another corner, Charlie was playing with empty shells and putting them into his mouth and spitting them out, then making a face. But he repeated that time and time again. A man was lying close to the fireplace, and there was a lot of blood around him.

Beckwourth said something in Crow to the Crow women, and they were so shocked he had finally spoken in their language that they froze in everything they were doing. He yelled at them again, and all hell broke loose. Two of the women came over and turned the wounded man on his back and showed the wounds to Immanuel. He left to get his horse and his saddlebags to make poultices.

The other two Crow women were helping Leah, but every once in a while, they would turn and look at Beckwourth. Finally, he went over to them and spoke gently in Crow and they both started crying, but continued to help Leah. Beckwourth then went over to the women who were cleaning Oscar's wounds and trying to wake him up. Beckwourth spoke to them in a sweet voice, and they, too, cried but kept working.

"I'm guessin' ya know who ya are, now?" Uzziah asked Beckwourth who looked at Uzziah and smiled and said, "I can't believe you and your partner read almost all those fucking boring journals to me!" But he was still smiling when he said, "Yes, I'm bloody arm, James Pierson Beckwourth, a war chief of the Crow Nation." He held out his forearm the way so many natives do, and as they clasped forearms, who should walk in but Immanuel!

"Okay, what the hell did I miss!?!"

"Never mind, make the poultices for this man," Beckwourth ordered, and Immanuel got right on it.

In twenty minutes, the poultices were made and the Crow women were applying them. Oscar had still not awakened, but Will was sitting right by his father's side with his little hands folded in prayer.

Immanuel pulled Uzziah aside. "What the hell, we're gonna let the son of a bitch go?"

"Don't have a clue, should we sneak out and go after him?"

"No, you should not," Beckwourth said. "He's desperate, and if we do not pursue now, he will not kill the woman."

"How do ya know?" Immanuel asked.

"Why would he take her when he escaped? If he just wanted to escape, he could have killed her first when all the confusion was going on. But he waited for that perfect moment of complete confusion and got the poor woman up and helped her to a horse. Of course, it was rather unceremonious how he put her on the horse, but it was expedient."

"What ya sayin'? He's in love with her?" Uzziah asked.

"Not in those terms, but he still wants her for himself, she must have presented him with a form of woman that he was not used to, men will do anything for that," Beckwourth said, then said some more to the two Crow women who were helping with the birth. Whatever he said, they put Leah up against the wall of the cabin with a blanket behind her and began pushing on her stomach. She cried out in pain.

"Stop them. They're hurting her!" Willet complained.

"Don't worry, the baby is almost here, and both will be fine," Beckwourth said to Willet, who calmed down immediately. It seemed this Beckwourth, the real Beck-wourth, had some power over men that neither Immanuel nor Uzziah had ever seen before. Later, Uzziah would say that that was how he imagined Jesus, able to quell the storms and all. Immanuel had said at the time, he sure as hell hoped that was like Jesus, because the Jesus he got taught was a pussy.

Beckwourth looked at both the mountain men, who looked like they would come out of their skins.

"We will catch the man, and the woman will be fine, she will be different, but fine."

Uzziah looked at Immanuel and shrugged, then both mountain men calmed down, that Beckwourth was something else.

Just then, there was a squalling from the other side of the cabin. "It's a girl," Willet said. "I have a daughter, by God!"

Uzziah and Immanuel went over and talked with the couple who had just become parents. The two Crow women slipped away and left them alone.

"Ophelia did the most amazing thing," Leah said. "She saved all our skins." She was talking fast as she held her daughter to her teat. All three men watched the nursing child and were glad to be able to. It was considered gracious when a woman nursed in public, and these men knew it.

"What exactly did she do?" Uzziah asked.

"Sit down, I'll tell ya both the whole story."

They sat and for the next hour they were regaled by a woman who could tell a good story, and who doesn't like a good story. She told them how Ophelia knew that the end was near for everybody, how she had changed into one of Leah's dresses and whored herself up, and gotten the whiskey from the root cellar, then bold as brass walked right out there without pantaloons on and challenged those men to a fuck! She then went on to tell how Ophelia regaled everyone with groans and moans and how she kept talking to them to get them to concentrate on her, how she turned the whole gangrape around on them, and really controlled all the men, and kept them from coming near the house.

Beckwourth was standing nearby, and when she got to that point, he said, "Standing Bear."

No one paid much attention to that, although Immanuel did get up and looked out the window to see if there was a standing bear out there. There wasn't.

Leah was crying and laughing and going on and on about her friend when Oscar awakened and heard some of the compliments that Leah was giving her female best friend.

"She's a whore!" he said as loud as he could, everyone turned to him and he passed out from the effort of those three words.

"And so it would seem to a man who does not understand," Beckwourth said.

"Understand what?" Immanuel asked.

"She was Standing Bear, protecting her cubs, her life meant nothing to her. They could shoot her, do nasty things to her, her story will live in the minds of these four Crow women for as long as they live."

———

Jimmy rode like hell, not worrying about how the woman felt, naked on the horse, thrown over it, and bouncing up and down. He didn't give a hoot! All he knew was he had to get away. He rode 'til the horse he was on was flecked with cottony sweat, and then he found a small stream that flowed under a small grove of cottonwood trees. The woman, he couldn't remember her name or even if she'd told them her name, that's what concerned him now, and he wasn't sure why. He got her off the horse and dumped her by the stream. She moaned and looked up at him.

"Clean yerself up, whore!" he yelled at her.

She was alive, and that was important. He had never known such a woman and probably never, ever would again in his time on this earth. For the first time in his life, he had found a woman who could take it like a man!

She spent a lot of time down by the stream. She was sore and her hands barely obeyed her wishes. When she walked up from the stream, he threw some old clothes of his saddlebags, they were dirty, but what would that matter?

"Dress yerself, ain't ya got no shame?!"

She dressed herself in them, and when she did, she saw that the place where they'd had their fun was raw.

"Got any of that Injun bear grease?" she asked him meekly.

"Just put on the clothes ifn ya wanna come by the fire, can't tolerate no naked whore by the fire," he said.

"Where are the rest of them sons a bitches?" she asked as she stepped into his pants.

"Dead, like you oughta be," was all he said.

"Why ain't you dead, ya bastard!" she spat out.

He stood and placed his cocked pistol against her forehead.

"Go on, ya lilly-livered, limp dick, do it!" she screamed and leaned into the barrel, actually pushing him backward while doing so.

"Ya think ya done seen the worst, but ya ain't, oh no, there's more than ya got back there comin' yer way," he said, uncocking his piece.

"I can hardly wait," she said and spat on him.

"Spit ain't gonna hurt me, better save it for that wounded quim 'cause I ain't done with it yet," he said, smiling an awful smile.

She squatted opposite the fire and warmed her hands, looking at him like no one had ever dared to look at him. He looked away,

———

Sometime in the middle of the night, he fell asleep, he was exhausted. When he awoke, the woman was making breakfast over a small fire. He worried about the smoke, but the cottonwoods broke it up. The bacon smelled good, and she kept looking at him with those mysterious eyes. He couldn't figure it out.

"Where'd ya get that chuck?" he asked her.

"Room service," she said sarcastically, and he didn't know quite what she meant.

He got up and went to the stream to pee, and when he came back, she had eaten all the bacon she'd cooked and was licking her fingers.

"Yer a fat, nasty whore," he said and when he moved toward her, she put her hands up like she knew how to fight. He laughed and put out the fire.

She watched him as he took the pans down to the stream and cleaned them the way an Injun would, using the sand as a scrubber. She hated everything about him, how he walked, how he stayed silent. God knew he'd said enough the night before.

What those men had done to her back there, what he had let them do to her, what he had done to her—it was all wrong, so very wrong. She would spend the rest of her life wondering if it had all been worth it. Maybe she should've just let them cut the baby out of Leah, kill her youngins, and shoot and kill their men. Maybe that would have been easier than what she had done to protect them. She was fairly sure she wouldn't be welcomed back at the settlement now, even if she got away. Well, at least the little boys, Will and Charlie, were still alive.

She had always wondered to herself why God had let her be raped the first time. She'd eventually stopped wondering, but now, she wasn't so sure whether God had anything to do with this last thing, that thing on the wagon, or whether the devil himself had gotten into her, and now she was his. The man there who had taken her from the settlement was nothing, just a man like a lot of men, full of hate for himself, which he took out on weaker creatures. Probably a dog kicker, too, she was sure of that! Sooner or later, he'd let down his guard, and when he did, he was a dead man, she knew that.

She was puzzled when no one was riding after them. Maybe they knew better, maybe Oscar had told them not to bother that he didn't want her anymore. Whatever the case, she was pleased that it looked like she could ride away with him without being tied up. She sat in his clothes on the horse and smelled his smell. It gagged her, but kept her ever vigilant. She would wipe that smell right off the face of the earth, that's one thing she was sure of. What happened after that was a blank, she'd probably kill herself. Well, it seemed the most logical thing to do.

7

When they found the campsite under the cottonwood trees, they were glad they were on the right trail. James Beckwourth was an excellent tracker, and if that wasn't enough, he had brought two of his Crow wives with him. They were so glad that he was back to being who he was before he'd been shot in the head, that each night as they camped, Uzziah and Immanuel had listened to them humping. First, one would crawl into his bedroll, then she would leave, and not fifteen minutes later, the other one would do the same. *If the night had been longer, well*, thought Immanuel, *if it had been winter, they never would have stopped crawling in and out of his bedroll.*

That morning, while Beckwourth and his two wives were at the stream cleaning themselves up, Uzziah turned to Immanuel.

"Ya suppose it's 'cause he's part Black that he can go on like that?"

"What ya talkin' 'bout fool, ifn I had those two beauties in my bedroll one after another, I'd have me a party and it wouldn't be in my pants," Immanuel said, sneaking a peek at the women when they'd taken their deerskin dresses off and were bathing.

"That ain't very nice," Uzziah reminded him.

"Whatcha talkin' 'bout, they is very nice, ya should take a look," Immanuel said, then turned his head quickly back to the breakfast that Uzziah was cooking.

"Got caught, didn't ya?" Uzziah said.

When the three of them came back from the stream, Beckwourth squatted down beside Immanuel. "Listen old son, if ya want one of them, just say so."

Immanuel looked at Beckwourth and smiled, but didn't say anything.

"I'll take that as a *no*," Beckwourth said, then he turned to Uzziah. "How 'bout you, young son?"

"It'd be my pleasure," Uzziah said, knowing that lots of chiefs, war or otherwise, shared their women.

"Then, tonight I'll send one to you. Which one would you prefer?" Beckwourth asked.

Uzziah looked around at the women, who couldn't have known what they were talking about because as far as he knew they didn't speak anything but Crow. "Makes no never mind to me," Uzziah said.

"Okay, good man," Beckwourth said.

As they were eating a breakfast of Uzziah's biscuits and bacon, Immanuel kept looking at Uzziah like he wanted to kill him or something.

After they'd cleaned up, and were back in the saddle, Immanuel rode up beside Uzziah. "Ya know he'll probably kill ya for wantin' one of his womens, young son."

"I don't think he will. I think he made ya a legit

offer, and ya turned the man and his womens down," Uzziah said, smiling.

"Yeah, well, when I find ya tomorra morning with a grim under yer chin, don't say I didn't warn ya," Immanuel grunted and rode away because Beckwourth had turned and was watching them from his saddle.

Uzziah realized that this man was probably the first man that Immanuel had ever feared in his life. It was making Immanuel act as if he weren't himself. What a pity when admiration, or even awe, can make a man act like that. Hadn't they brought the damn man back from the brink of never again knowing who he was? Hadn't they taken him to the site of where he would become *bloody arm* once again? Uzziah had known some admirable characters back in Virginia, but he always remembered what his mama's papa had told him, "They's put their pants on just the same as you and I," he had said.

That night, Beckwourth supposed that the criminal had taken the good woman into a town he knew of, which was about another day's ride away. They would arrive in that town about the same time that they'd arrived at the bloody massacre in the foothills of the Rockies. Beckwourth thought that it was auspicious that they would be able to kill him at the same time of day as his gang.

They ate dinner and Immanuel could not take his eyes off the Crow women, and he kept wondering to himself which one of those beauties would be the death of Uzziah?

They ate, Immanuel couldn't remember what they ate, but they ate. When they went to their bedrolls, Uzziah moved his bedroll a bit further away from Immanuel than he usually did, and Immanuel thought that was good, he wouldn't get the blood that drained from Uzziah's body all over his bedroll.

He wanted to stay awake and save his partner, even if it meant he had to kill Beckwourth, but the riding had tired him and he fell asleep.

Late in the night, or maybe it was near morning, he heard a sound, which did not mimic the sound of Beckwourth and his squaws. Then, he realized that something was happening to his partner, Uzziah. He was lurching up and down, probably from having his throat cut. He started to get up and try to save him, but then Uzziah's covers fell off the Crow woman, the younger of the two. Her breasts were bouncing nicely as she rode his partner like she rode her horse—hard! Her face was not a mask, but showed the pleasure that she and Uzziah were having, and he was just glad that he didn't have to see Uzziah's face, and all the gladness in it.

It was so titillating that he started to do something with his monkey, but decided that if Beckwourth caught him, he'd be exiled for sure.

The next morning, Immanuel woke up to a whistling Uzziah. He peeked from under his hat, and the man was grinning like he'd never seen him grinning before. God Almighty, was Immanuel pissed!

He got up and threw his covers away, and walked away to do his morning pissing. He heard the two Crow women talking, and the younger one was laughing and telling the other one something, and when he looked around, she had her hands out the way people do when they're describing the big fish they caught!

My God, thought Immanuel, *surely that couldn't be the length of his partner's thing-ama-gig!?! Could it?*

Beckwourth was all smiles and felicity with both men, but Immanuel was in a mood that was going to take some getting over. That was for sure.

"I saw y'all last night," Immanuel whispered to Uzziah when they'd gotten on the trail.

"Well, why didn't ya come over, there was plenty for both of us," Uzziah said, smiling.

"Yer kiddin'?"

"No, we shared the name that we do not say anymore, didn't we?"

"Well, yeah, but she was a—"

Uzziah put his hand out. "Do not say what you are about to say, my friend."

"Well, she was! Ya don't think the Crow woman woulda been upset?"

"Upset, those two women would have loved to have seen you get into the action, but now they mistakenly think yer too spirited!"

"What!?! Did ya set 'em straight?"

"How am I supposed to do that?"

"Son of a gun," Immanuel said, and he rode away from the partner who had taken what he wanted all along.

———

They reached the town near sunset, which, when you think about it, is about the same time of day as sunrise. It's the time when the terminus crosses the world and changes day to night or night to day, depending. But Beckwourth was happy that to him, those two times were interchangeable.

"I will ride into town and find this man," Beckwourth said.

"What about us?" Immanuel asked, and he didn't sound too friendly.

"This is about what your partner did with the younger Crow woman, isn't it?"

Immanuel knew he'd been discovered. "Yeah, it is," he admitted.

"Well, if you liked women, you would have had the same chance," Beckwourth said. "But we in the Crow Nation appreciate two-natured people, we understand," Beckwourth said with the kindest eyes Uzziah had ever seen. The man was not prejudiced.

"I ain't two nature, ya got that!" Immanuel said with some bite in it.

"To be one way and to deny it, is worse than being that way," Beckwourth said, putting his hand on Immanuel's shoulder.

Immanuel shrugged the hand off. "So, ya wantin' me to stay back 'cause ya think I'm two-natured, huh? That woman that he took was a friend of ours, she's the one I'm worried about, not yer feelings on rope suckers."

Beckwourth laughed out loud, turned to the two Crow women, and said something in Crow. They both looked at Immanuel and laughed good-naturedly.

"What the hell they laughin' at?!?"

"They like your description of the two natured spirit, rope sucking is very creative," Beckwourth said.

Now, Uzziah could see that no matter what

Immanuel said at this point, he was digging a hole that was getting deeper and deeper. So, he touched Immanuel, and when his partner turned to him, he simply shook his head, *no*.

"Fine!" Immanuel said. "But we's gonna go and shoot that son of a bitch full of holes whether ya want us there or not, ya get it?" Immanuel said as he walked toward his horse.

———

As all five of them, Uzziah, Immanuel, and Beckwourth and his two Crow wives got closer to the town, there was guitar music, Spanish guitar, if Uzziah wasn't mistaken, coming from one of the two saloons in the town. Both of them were right across the street from one another, which was strange, but not the first time Uzziah had seen such a thing.

They tied their horses up to the hitching post outside the saloon without the music and they—all three men, that is—walked up to the batwing doors, and Beckwourth stopped short of going in, looking over the top of the batwings.

"'Cuse me," Immanuel said as he blew past Beckwourth and entered the saloon.

"He's got a problem, doesn't he?" Beckwourth said out loud, and Uzziah wasn't sure he was being asked, so he let it go.

Beckwourth followed Immanuel in and Uzziah was behind him.

All three men ended up at the bar, bellied up to it, as it were. Beckwourth order a whiskey, and so did

Immanuel. Uzziah kept it to a beer, which was frothy and cool.

After serving Uzziah, the barkeep kept drying his hands on the bar towel he carried in his apron strings.

"Jest passin' through?" he asked in a high squeaky voice. Beckwourth ignored him as he was checking out the other patrons.

Uzziah had been taught to respect older people, and since the man was at least in his sixties and hobbling a bit, he spoke up.

"Yeah, sorta," Uzziah said, taking another sip from the beer. "Beer's cool, that's good."

The old man evidently did not like being ignored by the mulato, so he pressed his point. "Either yer passin' through or ya ain't," he said louder, suspecting that the mulato might be partially or completely deaf.

Again, Beckwourth ignored him, although he was looking directly at him.

"Ya deaf?" the old man asked Beckwourth right to his face.

"And he can't read lips, neither," Uzziah said.

"Well, hell, that explains a lot, thought the nigger was ignorin' me!"

At that, Beckwourth reached across the bar and with his arm completely stretched out, he picked up the old man by the throat and held him while he squirmed and kicked. Finally, he set the old man down as he gasped for breath.

"Who has just arrived in town?" he asked the old man as he caught his wind.

"You, you, and you," the old man said, pointing to each of them in turn.

"Right before us, right before?"

"The man with the deaf-mute woman," the old barkeep said, rubbing his neck.

"And where would they be?"

"At the hotel, waiting to be wed," the old geezer said.

"Thank ye," Beckwourth said and downed the shot of rye, then flipped a twenty-dollar gold piece to the man, who deftly caught it and smiled in spite of his wrenched neck.

"No, no thank ye, thank ye much," he screeched as they walked from the saloon.

The night had finally won over the day. There wasn't a hint of the sun in the west, and clouds scudded by under a partially waning moon. An eagle flew by and was circled by the waning moon, and he tipped his wings slightly and was gone. Uzziah couldn't help but think how when we make decisions, even little ones, it was the tipping of our eagle's wings. Sometimes the stakes are so high, and the situation so dire, that a little tip is enough to send us plummeting to earth, unheeding of the approaching prairie which looms up beneath us.

He thought about that as they crossed the street and went further down to the only hotel in town. Maybe it wasn't too late for Ophelia to pull out of the downward spiral she had tipped herself into, and then again, maybe it was, and she had gone too far in her wheeling and turning. He would have to wait and see how it played out.

"You got a couple here that are getting married tomorrow?" Beckwourth asked the man behind the desk.

"Sure do, lovely couple, preacher's got them lined up for ten a.m. tomorrow morning, are you boys part of the wedding party?"

"We are, can we get a room next to theirs?"

"One room fer three fellas?"

"I like the floor, they'll take the bed," Beckwourth said, and he paid for the room in advance, which was customary.

As they clunked up the wooden stairs, their boots echoing off the bare walls of the lobby, Immanuel started in, "We gonna take 'em tonight?"

"No, tomorrow at the wedding," was all Beckwourth said.

"What about yer two wives?" Uzziah asked.

"Send them up the backway, I'm sure there is one, then you two meet us at the church in the morning," he said as he got to room nine. They were in ten. Without much trouble, they could hear rutting going on in ten.

"He's at her again," Immanuel said. "I don't like it!"

"Neither does she, but it's his last meal, so to speak," Beckwourth said, then added, "There's the backway in. Send my wives up now," and he went in and closed the door behind him.

Immanuel and Uzziah went down the backway, Immanuel grumbling all the while.

They gathered the two Crow women, escorted them up to room nine, and then went back down.

"I don't have to tell ya this, but I don't like it, I don't like it one bit!" Immanuel was saying on their way to their horses. They gathered up Beckwourth's horses, all three of them, and took them down to the hostler, who was glad for the two bits.

"I saw a nice site just as we came in, there's a spring

and everything," Uzziah said, handling this better than his partner. He wasn't worried about anything or anyone but Ophelia. He couldn't help but think of the most famous Ophelia, Hamlet's girlfriend and Polonius's daughter. She had gone insane with Hamlet's indecision, and in the end, well before the end of the play, drowned herself beneath a weeping willow tree.

Uzziah was right as always about the camping site. It was choice, and it didn't cost them a cent.

"Ya wants me to make some supper?" he asked Immanuel.

"I ain't hungry, I ain't ever hungry when I'm angry."

Uzziah built a small fire and made coffee. They sat around drinking it, watching the lights in town go out.

"Why do ya suppose he wants us to wait?" Immanuel asked thoughtfully over his second cup.

Uzziah really didn't feel like answering that question, but he felt he owed it to Immanuel.

"They's in there humping and ifn we barged in, well, Ophelia might get shot, and how she's stayed alive this long is anybody's guess."

"Well, I know why, they told us. She lured them into a sex party, and now she's placating the monster who's humping her some more."

"It'll all come out in the wash," Uzziah said.

"That's one of yer ma's sayings, ain't it?"

"Yeah, it is, and she was nearly always right," Uzziah said, putting the fire out.

"What ifn I wanted more coffee?!" Immanuel asked angrily.

"There's plenty in the pot, it'll stay warm fer hours sitting on the coals," Uzziah said and rolled into his bedroll. The smell inside the bedroll reminded Uzziah of the pleasuring that he'd been treated to the night before. Strange how man turned good things into bad things by just not being able to wait. Immanuel was suffering from an unusual state of impatience, and Uzziah didn't think it had anything to do with either Ophelia or the man who was thrusting himself into her in room 10. It was a personal problem now disguised as something quite outside Immanuel, but it wasn't outside, it was within the very heart of the man he loved and called his partner.

The few times Uzziah woke up, Immanuel was talking low to himself, and he just got up and peed, or rolled over and went back to sleep. *No sense in antagonizing a wounded bear*, thought Uzziah.

———

The next morning, Immanuel was not in his bedroll, but had collapsed by the fire, well, the coals. The pot of coffee was gone, so he traipsed down to the stream and filled the pot again and built the coals back up into a good fire.

It was getting fairly late when Uzziah poked Immanuel. "It's nine-thirty, partner."

Immanuel grumbled and ate a biscuit with some bacon on it, and drank a couple cups of coffee, then they were off to the church for the wedding.

When they got even with the hotel, Beckwourth was waiting around back and he rode out with his two Crow wives.

"We'll wait until the service has started afore we go

in," he said, and the two mountain men grunted their approval.

They could hear the organ wheezing away for dear life when they tied their horses up in front. They walked into the church, and the bad hombre, they still didn't know his name, and Ophelia were standing up front. He had found her a dress, they were to find out later that it belonged to the preacher's wife, and Ophelia looked tolerable in it.

Then the preacher started in, "Dearly beloved. We are gathered here today in God's presence to join together this man and woman. If there is anybody here who has any reason to believe that this couple should not be wed, let them speak now, or forever hold their peace." He was about to go on when Beckwourth spoke up.

"I believe they should not be joined together," he said, and both Jimmy and Ophelia turned to see who had spoken, and when Ophelia saw both Immanuel James Jones and Uzziah Ferguson O'Bannon standing there, something snapped in her.

"Argh!" She made a sound like a wounded animal, then, quick as a wink, drew Jimmy's knife from its scabbard and plunged it into his chest. He looked down at the knife, knowing it was his, and wishing he hadn't made it so sharp. He looked at the preacher and reached out to him, and the preacher ran from the church like it were a game of tag. His wife, who had played the wheezing organ and pumped herself into a near sweat, slid down between the organ and the seat, whimpering like a beat puppy.

Jimmy's eyes were the size of saucers as he, with a great deal of effort, reached for his pistol. Ophelia took her fists and joined them together like she was about to pray. She raised them above her head and spoke to Jimmy, who was in shock and still playing with getting his pistol out, all the while staring at the knife in his chest.

"Yer a no-good asswipe, and I will see ya in hell!" she shouted in his face, then she brought the heels of both hands down so hard her feet left the floor, thwacking the hilt of the knife as hard as she could, driving it halfway to his heart, then raising her prayerful hands again she whacked it again, sinking it to the hilt.

He looked down at the knife one more time and fell over backward, hitting the boards of the church floor so hard, he bounced up, then settled into his death, all the air escaping from him in bloody bubbles on his lips.

Ophelia took one last hateful look, then ran from the church, and Beckwourth stood in Immanuel and Uzziah's way of going to her.

"My wives will see to her," was all he said.

Outside, she was wrestling with the Crow wives of Beckwourth, but they were handling her just fine. Eventually, she broke into tears and fell into their arms.

———

Ophelia rode double with one of the Crow women, and when they went to the hostlers, they got her horse, plus the horribly treated horse of Jimmy's.

The hostler wanted payment.

"You can have that horse," Beckwourth said, and after looking the horse over, the man agreed. Uzziah and Immanuel both knew that with the proper treatment and feed, the horse would look great.

As they rode along, Ophelia would not look at anyone but the Crow women. They talked to her constantly, and when they camped at night, they made their own fire and would not mingle with the men.

"What's goin' on?" Immanuel asked.

"Healing," was all Beckwourth offered.

They traveled extremely slow, half the usual distance for a party of men. But Beckwourth would offer no explanations. About the fifth night out, there was singing at the woman's campfire, and Immanuel got up and started in that direction.

"Don't," Beckwourth said.

"I'm sick and tired of you telling us what to do," Immanuel said, and continued on his way to see what the women were doing.

"It's just you who needs the telling," Beckwourth commented, but Immanuel kept on.

About halfway there, he was tackled by Beckwourth, who only subdued him by holding his arms down. Uzziah realized then just how strong Beckwourth was.

"I am not telling you both what to do, Uzziah knows better. It is you that I am having trouble with. You must trust the women for all of them have been raped and abused before they married me. They know about abuse and how to heal that woman's soul. If you interfere, she will go mad with grief and self-abuse. They are recreating her."

"Get up, I won't go over there, but get off me!" Immanuel demanded.

Beckwourth got off him and Immanuel jumped up.

"Your anger is at the man who did this to her, and

even he is beyond it. You must relax and let the Crow way work."

Immanuel was restless that night and hardly slept by Uzziah's standards. But when they got ready to ride out, and they looked at the women who had mounted up, they were confused. Now, instead of two Crow women, there were three.

Ophelia was dressed in traditional Crow dress, just as Beckwourth's wives. She had on a white buckskin shirt and leggings with beadwork, three lines of it down her sleeves, and at the cuff a circle of beads and fringe dangling down. Her hair was bound up in leather with braids on either side of her face, and each braid was fastened with a beaded brooch. In her hand, just like Beckwourth's Crow Wives, she carried an eagle feather fan, and her moccasins were laced up on the outside with beadwork squares, three of them on each legging.

"So now ya got three wives?" Immanuel protested.

"No, now there are three Crow women riding with us, not two," Beckwourth said and left it at that.

———

It took them almost a month to get back to the settlement. The little baby girl who had been born to Leah was big and fat, and they all came out to see who was riding in.

Oscar hung back, and when the other two wives of Beckwourth ran out to greet their sisters, they cele-brated the new woman of the Crow Nation by the ululation of their tongues, and even Ophelia ululated.

"Where's my wife? Where's Ophelia?" Oscar demanded.

"She died on the trail back here," Beckwourth said, but Oscar walked out and looked at the third Crow woman.

"Ophelia, is that you!?" he demanded.

She spoke to him in Crow. It certainly wasn't the best Crow anyone had ever spoken, but it was Crow, and the other women surrounded her and smiled at her as she talked to Oscar.

"What have you done to my wife Ophelia!? What!?!" Oscar screamed at the three men, then he took his rifle, jumped on his horse, and disappeared over the first ridge.

That night, they had a celebration with Willet, Leah, the newborn, Will, and Charlie.

The boys knew that this beautiful Crow woman was their mother, and like all children, they did not care that she had decided to be someone new. As far as they were concerned, she was pretending as they often did when they played together. There was no difference in her except her pretense, and they celebrated that along with everyone else.

———

Three months passed, and still Oscar Blanchard had not returned. Standing Bear, that's what Ophelia was now called because she stood as a mother bear would stand to protect her cubs, taught both Leah, Willet, and the children how to speak Crow, well, how to speak what Crow she knew. Later in their lives, this knowledge would save them from almost certain death. By the time Oscar returned, he had expected his wife Ophelia to have dressed as she was before, and taken her place in the family. She had not changed back though, and never again spoke the language of her birth.

Beckwourth listened well to all the Crow women and learned much. He told what he had learned to Uzziah, Willet, and Immanuel. Oscar refused to listen.

"Grandmother Earth is above all things, and created all things. She is above all things, yet she is within all things. In everything they do, they are in contact with Grandmother Earth. They say the women who made the men look away from her cubs died in doing that. That is why she is called Standing Bear. She was a target for the men and nothing more. The men who were diverted from their destruction of her cubs shot into her, and with those shots destroyed her. The former woman has been broken and cannot be put together again as she once was. She is now Standing Bear, a new person, who will continue to protect and defend her family, but now, she will do this from the perspective of a Crow woman."

They guessed Oscar had heard enough, even if he was standing away from them, because he got back on his horse and rode away.

"Are we gonna go back up fer the winter, partner?" Immanuel asked after the explanation of what had happened to the woman who had once lived here.

"I'd kinda like to help them rebuild. They can't all live in that one cabin, and there's a lot of work to be done," Uzziah said.

"Well, I think you're right, and what's more, I think I've been wrong about a whole bunch of stuff."

"Oh yeah?"

"Yeah, like when I was in awe of James Pierson Beckwourth, why he's no better or worse than any of us, and now, I see, he's simply a good man with different ways."

Uzziah didn't press that since he knew that Immanuel was still butt hurt about the women thinking he was double spirited, but he just hugged his partner and let it go at that.

8

They did stay, and another larger cabin was rebuilt with a lot of muscle from Beckwourth and the two mountain men. When the first snow came, Oscar Blanchard returned ready to live with his wife who had become a Crow, but when he saw her belly, he didn't know what to do.

"She's pregnant!" he yelled indignantly at Uzziah and Immanuel.

"Yeah, yeah, she is," Uzziah said, looking with compassion on a man who not only had to get used to his wife not being exactly herself again, but now she was going to have a baby.

Immanuel brought a jug out and he, Beckwourth, Uzziah, and Oscar got fairly drunk.

"Ya know what really gets me?" Oscar asked about two and a half sheets to the wind.

"What?" asked Beckwourth.

"She weren't even raped, she went out there with those men carrying two bottles of whiskey and she spread 'em for them, that's what really gets me!"

"And would ya rather have been butchered by those same men?" Immanuel asked.

"Of course not, I mean, shit, I know she saved our bacon givin' y'all time to get here, but hell, man, I could hear her callin' fer them to have at her quim! What kinda woman does that??!"

"A really brave one," Uzziah said, and knew that wasn't going to sit well, but Oscar just looked at his friend Uzziah and broke down into sobs.

"*Ex vino veritas*," Beckwourth said.

"*Out of wine comes the truth*," Immanuel translated.

————

As it turned out, at one point, Uzziah thought that Immanuel would ride off with Beckwourth and his four wives when they left. And, given all that had happened, Uzziah figured if that was the way it was going to be, then that was the way it was going to be.

Beckwourth really liked Immanuel's company and the two learned men talked incessantly into many nights, subjects which Uzziah knew nothing about and didn't care to know anything about.

Oscar finally moved back into the new cabin with his now Crow wife, and he was there when a baby boy was born, and to everyone's unexpected pleasure, the boy was the spitting image of Oscar. She was pregnant the night she went out and was Standing Bear to protect her cubs, even her unborn one.

Oscar was gracious when he realized his ignorance and treated her like a Crow Queen after that. She taught him Crow and the boys, too, and they named the little one Cubby.

When it came on spring and it was time for everyone to go their own ways, Immanuel realized that no matter how much he enjoyed Beckwourth's company, he had a partner that he would never leave. A man who had been taught by him to be what he was today, a mountain man by the name of Uzziah Ferguson O'Bannon.

Beckwourth, his four Crow wives, and Uzziah and Immanuel left the same day. Beckwourth down to the Santa Fe, where he'd been headed when he'd been waylaid by Johnny and his gang, and Immanuel and Uzziah back up to their mountain cabins.

Something had been forgotten with the advent of modernity. Something which these three men would never have dreamed of. A man's way would be forgotten, and those about him would also forget that to be someone of consequence, all one had to do was follow his heart. It's as simple and as difficult as that.

The ride to their cabins was uneventful, and they decided on the way to go and see the land of the burning grounds. After all, hadn't they said goodbye to Abooksigun as he had gone to see the same grounds? True, Immanuel had been there, but there was something about seeing something through another man's eyes that would make the journey worthwhile.

When they got there, it was truly amazing. The land of vapors was vaporing and Immanuel told Uzziah all he learned about it, and they camped near streams which were burning hot, and swam in other cool clear streams, and as fall was approaching, they packed up and started to leave when they saw back in the woods, an old teepee situated close to the one of the vapors which would later be called Old Faithful.

They rode in making lots of noise, and as they got closer, the flap to the teepee was pushed back, and who should be standing there but Abooksigun.

"You trackin' me?" he asked, and they laughed about that.

Sitting in the teepee that night, Abooksigun had fixed them a deer meat Indian stew, and as they ate fry bread and dipped the stew from wooden bowls, Abooksigun told them why he was still there. "Only comin' to see," he said.

"But ya stayed," Uzziah said.

"Yes."

"Why?"

"Not sure, but vapors talk to me," he admitted, looking down into his bowl.

"What do they say?" Immanuel asked.

"Trouble understanding, but always speaking."

"So, yer not leavin' 'til ya do?" Uzziah asked.

"Like that, yes," Abooksigun said.

"Well, they say they're enchanted," Immanuel said.

"I believe that."

"We still got four cabins up Rockies way," Uzziah said, implying the question that if he wanted to come with them.

"What do of likeness?"

"The one my ma drew?" Uzziah asked.

"That one, yes."

Immanuel left the teepee and came back with it and the one Rahab had done of him. He handed Abooksigun the drawing Rahab had done of the Indian.

"Still me, hasn't changed," Abooksigun said. "What that one?"

Immanuel didn't bother to explain, he just handed the drawing to the Algonquin Injun.

Abooksigun opened it, and looked at it a long time, turning it this way and that, until Immanuel got uneasy.

"Why no clothes?"

Immanuel shrugged.

"She drew everyone like that," Uzziah explained, then realized she hadn't drawn Abooksigun that way.

"I see."

They sat there in silence, an uneasy silence for about ten minutes, then Abooksigun eyes brightened.

"I no clothes, too, but she draw, sparing lesser men," he said, and it was probably the longest sentence they had ever heard him speak. He looked very serious, and neither Uzziah nor Immanuel knew what to say.

"You two no get it, huh?" Abooksigun finally said.

There were shouts of laughter as all three enjoyed his dry sense of humor.

The next day, they left and as they were standing outside the tent, mounted up, Abooksigun tilted his head toward one of the hot springs.

"Are they talkin' to ya?" Uzziah asked.

"No, to you, say goodbye," he said and was still laughing when they rounded a bend in the trail.

———

Summer had ended, and fall was announcing itself on the higher peaks with snow which wouldn't melt 'til next spring.

It was Gaius Plinius Secundus, a Roman Philosopher who said, *"Home is where the heart is,"* and he said it a good two thousand years before Immanuel James Jones and Uzziah Ferguson O'Bannon rounded the last bend, and the cabins came into view.

Those who have never had a home cannot imagine the joy those simple boards and beams made in the hearts of those two mountain men. And yet, surely there had to be out there in this great and lovely world a place that everyone could call home, no?

There was a pigeon waiting with a missive from the settlement. It had these words written in Leah's hand, *We wish you well, as all is well.*

A LOOK AT BOOK FOUR:
BUFFALO RUN
A UZZIAH MOUNTAIN MAN WESTERN DOUBLE

Blood on the trail. Justice in their sights.

When a message leads Uzziah O'Bannon and Immanuel Jones to legendary frontiersman Jim Beckwourth, the two mountain men are swept into a historic buffalo run in Montana Territory. But what begins as an adventure turns deadly fast—tribal tensions boil over, a boy is kidnapped, and war looms between rival nations. As Immanuel rides into danger to rescue the child, Uzziah tries to keep the peace—and keep them both alive.

Back at the settlement, a bloodied tinker wagon rolls in with a dark tale of women stolen by Comancheros. The rescue turns tragic, and when two young girls fall back into enemy hands, Uzziah and Immanuel give chase—straight into a storm of murder, misunderstanding, and a brutal showdown in Anton Chico.

Caught between slavers, ranchers, and the law, the mountain men must decide what justice means in a land where the innocent are sold, and a man's life is worth the lead in his holster.

This two-book bundle includes the seventh and eighth novels in the Uzziah Mountain Man series.

AVAILABLE NOVEMBER 2025

ABOUT THE AUTHORS

He was good looking and could sell ice to eskimos. But ... writing asked something else from him. He would have to corral his interest in being free. Writing would take him to a place where he was tamed, but also able to actually tell a story.

After the first two weeks at the Yale School of Drama, he called the head of the playwriting department, Milan Stitt and told him he was quitting. Milan invited him to lunch at a nearby Mexican restaurant in New Haven. He told the man who had had plays on Broadway that he wanted to be a free writer. Milan smiled, then explained the way to freedom was always through discipline.

Something in him clicked and it all began to make sense.

Three years later, when he received his MFA in playwriting, he received the much coveted Cole Porter Prize for Excellence in Writing.

Enter a woman, years later, when the first 'J' in J.J. Bonham, Jack Bonham, had written thirty screenplays in 7 years and had one optioned which looked like it actually might be done.

Unlike Milan Stitt, this woman had no plays on Broadway, but was a divorced mother of four grown children. She loved soaps, and was an ardent watcher of the same. In the years of her devotion to watching she developed an uncanny ability to discern plot and analyze character. Uncanny, really better than any of his teachers at Yale.

They, Jack & Judy, the other 'J' in J.J. Bonham, married in Buffalo Springs, Colorado. While teaching elementary school in Denver they read the same novella and looking up and into each other's eyes, realizing something. They could do that.

Thirteen years later they had written nearly 200 novels. Westerns mostly because that was who they were – a misplaced couple from the 19th Century who saw life in a western justice sort of way. They danced in Virgina City, Montana. Dances from a different time and place, but still their time and place.

Now, they live in the Bitterroot Valley on five acres and looking out the office window as he puts this together for them, he can see the thunderstorm marching across the Sapphire Mountains. Earlier, sitting on the porch, she had said something about the crack of lightning years before as they said vows of love in Buffalo Springs. He remembered.